STAB THE REMOTE

D1297693

Copyright © 2021 Kurt Eisenlohr
Published Exclusively and Globally by Far West Press

All rights reserved. No part of this book may be reproduced
without written permission from the publisher or author, with
the exception of passages used in critical essays and reviews.

This is a work of fiction. All names, characters, organizations,
and events are either the products of the author's imagination or
used in a fictitious manner.

Some of the stories in this book originally appeared in the
following publications: *Air in the Paragraph Line, Dark Sky
Magazine, Horror Sleaze Trash, Unlikely 2.0,* and *Smokebox.*

Cover illustration: Kurt Eisenlohr

Subjects: LCSH: Working class—Fiction. Working poor—
Fiction.

www.farwestpress.com
First Edition
ISBN 978-1-7365388-5-2
Printed in the United States of America

for JR

Clock

I don't live alone, I have two cats. They're getting old, though, and I'm afraid.

I open a can of tuna, spoon it into two bowls. Put the bowls on the floor.

My heart is full of love for you.

It's happening so fast now.

Two Little Nixon Ears

I move around most days with the feeling that I am already dead. I walk through streets and life and nothing registers. I feel encased in surgical gauze: thick, heavy, muted, hopeless. I'm always tired. All I want to do is sleep. But I have to pay the rent, which means I have to go to work, which means I have to keep getting out of bed, shaving, brushing my teeth, gagging, getting dressed, getting on the bus, breathing in and out—a dazed alien in a numb human body.

It's when you do the same thing every day that you begin to die.

In India there's a baby with a tail who is worshiped as a god. I don't have a tail, and freaks are scorned in America—that type, anyway. Americans prefer Tom Cruise and Anna Nicole Smith, serial killers, Kardashians.

What I want is a tail, and to live in India.

It's what you want, too, in your own special way.

I'm at work one day, tending bar. I'm waiting tables, running food, doing dishes. Three different people are pawing me all at once. They literally have their hands on me. One wants ranch, another wants beer, one wants to know where the bathroom is. It's one of those moments when you see yourself from a slight distance—detached, and far too clearly—as if watching yourself from above. It's a movie, a surveillance tape, your own two little Nixon ears. What does that mean? Your guess is as good as mine. Two little Nixon ears. I like the sound of it. It has a ring, nice and ominous. Every day I worked there I could feel the life going out of me a little more. Server, servant—they sound so similar because they are, and they both sound a bit like...best not think about it too much.

So the years roll by and I'm forty and my new thing is greeting customers with the word "die." Say a morbidly obese woman routinely makes me run like a 1930s houseboy back and forth for more tartar more cocktail more butter more diet Coke—always with a snap. She walks through the door and I say, Die. She says, What? And I say, Hi.

Oh, I thought you said die!

That's a bit morbid, don't you think?

I guess I'm feeling insecure today, sorry about that.

And I seat her, and wonder what the hell is wrong with me, with her, with the world. And just when I think I have it figured out, I realize I know nothing, understand nothing, and my eyes well up.

Why are you crying?

My dad died.

When?

Twenty years ago.

See what I mean?

Self-Generating Suspect Email Poem

Put an end to ugly skin tags
Update your profile
Get the lowest prices on vehicles
Attract your perfect mate
Entry pending
Member exclusive
Hot Stone Massage
A nation of rape
Remember

Where Did You Go?

He's wearing dog tags and a faded UNICEF t-shirt, loads of cologne yet giving off a death-stench underneath (or on top of), sweating, grimacing, twitching, spit drying at the corners of his mouth, sitting in his own shit, or somebody else's.

It's me (very high) and the driver and this guy, no one else on the bus, the three of us parked here together on a twelve minute layover. Dead silence save the ticking of the engine as it cools...I'm thinking good thoughts...tick...I'm thinking good thoughts...tick...Then compulsion drops the needle down and the record begins to play.

"So I got a five dollar haircut at the barber school today," the guy says, and I lip sync along. He runs his hands over his head while swaying in his seat. "It's no good," he says, my lips moving with his. "I feel like I'm back in the Marine Corp! Goddamnit!"—(My lips moving)—"GODDAMNIT!" He puts his face in his hands, falls forward at the waist and begins to rock rapidly back and forth while moaning. The driver and I lock eyes in the rear-view mirror but the driver immediately breaks it. Bad luck, right there—seven years worth. The five dollar haircut guy, his fists are clenched so tight they're trembling.

"Goddamnit...GODDAMNIT!"

I open the *New York Times*. Op-Ed section: *War*. Business section: *War*. Sports: *War*. Thursday Styles...

"FUCKING MARINE CORP HAIRCUT!"

I hide in the *Times*. The driver clears his throat. "We make our own reality," he announces over the intercom. "You guys report it, we make it."

"What?" I half-shout the question.

"One of Bush's boys said that to a reporter last week."

"Oh, I thought you were talking to me."

"I am talking to you."

"FUCKING STUDENT BARBERS!"

I can't concentrate. I fold the *Times* and put it back in my bag.

Five dollar haircut guy wrestles his shirt off, throws it at me. I hook it with the toe of my shoe and kick it back to him.

We do this at least once a week.

The bus begins to move.

I look out the window and see an old man with a shopping cart full of trash standing in the middle of a crosswalk, channeling traffic. He's a small dying sun. We nearly run him over, or rather, the driver does. On purpose, I suspect, though I can't be certain.

Five dollar haircut guy yanks the cord, the bell dings, the driver stops and the doors fly open. Five dollar haircut guy bails.

The driver asks me, "Are you on or off?"

"I'm on," I tell him.

And off we go. I'm going to a bar. The driver's going in circles. That's his job. My job, too, I guess.

I'm parked at the dark end of the bar in George's Tavern, drinking a hot toddy. I'm sick, slightly feverish, reading the paper—DOOM, it still reads—when the other (another) approaches...Long denim hair, cowboy hat, stash.

"I'm fucking starving," he tells me. "I can't believe you charge three dollars for a corn dog. Come on, man! I got enough for this beer, not even a tip. No, wait, I got a quarter, I got this fucking quarter." He slams it on the bar. "There you go. That's all I got. I can't even afford a fucking corn dog!"

"What?"

"You own the joint, don't you?"

"No."

"Don't bullshit me, you're the owner, I can tell."

"Dude, if I owned a bar I'd be dead. I'm not the owner, trust me."

"Alright," he laughs. "That's a good one. I like you."

A good one? I go back to reading the paper. I'm thinking it's a good one I don't have a car, kids, house, a mortgage to pay. For the first time in my life I'm thinking it's good I don't have much of anything. I've never even had a credit card. I carry no debt. Does that make me rich, or blatantly un-American?

He sits down next to me, Three Dollar Corn Dog Guy.

"You in a band?" he asks.

"No."

"Come on, man. What band are you in?"

"I'm not in a band, dude."

"No, man, really, what do you play, guitar? You're a guitarist, I can tell."

"I don't play."

"You look like a guitar player. Look like a damn good one, too."

"I don't play guitar."

"You got an old lady?"

"Yeah," I tell him. It's true. I do have an old lady. But she's fourteen years younger than I am. I'm going to lose her, just like I lost my wife. That's why I'm here so often. I should be home with her now but I'm not. I haven't been home in years. I'll sit there with her sometimes and disappear into myself. I'll fall in so deep I can't reach out. "Where do you go?" she asks. I wish I knew. I need to know.

"*Ah*—she made you quit, didn't she?"

"I don't play."

"Yes you do!"

"What the fuck is wrong with you?"

"Tell the old lady to eat shit! Fuck it—let's get the band back together!"

"What band?"

"The fucking *band*, man! You played bass for the Eagles, right?

"The Eagles?"

"Yeah, man, the Eagles! That's you on the back of those album covers!"

"The *Eagles*?"

"You're too modest. Let me buy you a drink."

"You're broke."

"Well, buy me a drink, then."

"Do I look like I have money?"

"Yeah, you do."

I buy the guy a drink.

I get up, pretending to piss, walk exactly fourteen steps to the bathroom, turn, take a detour, open a door and disappear into the night.

I've forgotten my newspaper.

A sharp dressed Black dude standing by the Burger King on

the corner of 4th and Burnside: old school inner city jazz fashionista with a dash of Super Fly. I may or may not give him a nod as I pass him by.

"You straight?" he asks, silver hair catching the streetlight.

"I'm cool." I keep walking. It's 2 a.m., people sleeping on the sidewalk, in doorways, plastic bags, their shoes, a few crack-heads being way too obvious, a cop car or four. I'm on my way to Cal-Sport, drunk, hell-bent on making last call.

"You sure, man?"

I can feel him back there, radar clocking my itch, his shoes rapping the sidewalk as he tracks me.

I stop, turn to face him. "What's up?"

"I got a problem."

"Yeah?"

"I got six OxyContin I gotta get rid of. I gotta walk through the drug free zone to get home."

"I don't have the money."

"How much you got?"

"Not enough."

"Fifty bucks, man. It's a fire sale."

"I only have seven." Seven bills folded in my front pocket, my wallet elsewhere.

"Oh, come on, man! They're 40s!"

"Seven is all I have."

"You're crazy."

"It's all I have." I start to walk.

He grabs me by the shoulder, lets go. "Listen, there's some Klonopin in here too." Pulls a little glass tube from his vest pocket, shakes it.

"Klonopin? That shit's for squares."

He gets a laugh out of that. Looks around for cops, shakes his head. "Okay, old school, for you, seven."

I give him the money. He hands me the tube full of pills. They're either allergy tabs or I've lucked, almost indecently, into the best deal in the world. He's still laughing.

"Thanks," I tell him.

"No sweat. I'll see you around."

I put the pills in my pocket and make a beeline through the Drug Free Zone—I'm white in an overwhelmingly white, segregated city, on no cop shop list—to Cal-Sport. I'm half hoping someone tries to kill me. I'm ready. I think I'm ready. But no one does.

Before I enter, I stop and check. It's too dark to tell if they're real or not—same with the girl on the sidewalk. I step through the door, duck into the bathroom to be sure.

Joe is sitting at the bar. He's smart, owns his cab. When he wants a night off, he leases it out to drivers who don't own cabs. He still makes money, sitting in the bar, drinking beer.

"Joe."

"Mister Sandman, hello."

I order a draft. I fish the tube from my pocket, dangle it in Joe's face.

"What are those?"

I widen my eyes.

"Let me see one." he says.

"Twenty bucks," I tell him. I know he's not interested. "I'm kidding. Buy me this beer, though. I'm out of cash. Is the ATM machine working?

"Yeah, they fixed it."

I give Joe two different pills to inspect, and walk over to the ATM machine. I get the card in there. After three tries I get the PIN number right. A twenty comes jumping out of the slot—cab fare. I sit back down next to Joe.

"What are these?" he says.

"Pain killers, Klonopin."

"I'm not in pain."

"Anxious?"

"Nope."

"Then give them back."

"Don't do those all at once," he says.

I gulp my beer and leave. On the way out I announce into the night (key of E), "If you do these all at once, you'll die," my voice echoing back at me from beneath the Steel Bridge. I kneel and press the pills into the hand of the whack-shack model I know, knew, used to be friends with a lifetime ago, still sitting near the door, on the sidewalk, weeping. She holds the tube to the smeared streetlight, shakes it, casting a spell on herself, staring at the pills inside.

"If you do those all at once, you'll die," I tell her, the words drawn all around us, cartoon thought bubbles in the polluted

13

air.

"I heard you the first time," she says.

"I wasn't talking to you the first time."

"You were singing," she says. "It's nice to hear you sing."

I linger, lulled by the sound of traffic, a vision of the ocean eighty miles to the west of us. The ocean. I once nearly drowned in it. Pulled from the water by unseen hands, the breath of angels filling my lungs. Being alive felt electric.

Incident Report

Wake up (2 p.m.)

Piss.

Nuke coffee (16 oz.) Drink it while smoking cigarettes.

Scribble in blank book/cut & paste.

Get high, look out window at mountain.

Back to blank book, more coffee, cigarettes.

Call a girl named Anna who found my wallet in her cab. "You were really drunk that night," she tells me. I must have been blacked out, because I don't remember her driving me home. I thought an old German guy drove me. Chester? A ghost? I get my nights confused. I wonder if she's cute. I love her voice. Her voice is cute. She says she's going to leave my wallet at Radio Cab Headquarters.

Blank book, cigarettes—puff again?

Brush teeth, wash face, dress.

Look for CDs to sell.

Take bus to Django's, sell CDs ($34.00)

Eat two items from the dollar menu at McDonald's.

Buy pack of American Spirits ($4.95).

Drop off roll of film at Freddie's ($10.00) (fuck!)

6:15 p.m.

Currently drinking a can of Hamm's ($1.25) at the Matador, and waiting. Waiting for what?

Pills

I've always had a thing for pills. It started in high school. It was real easy to buy pharmaceutical speed in 1979. There were these older guys who sold them by the football field. Yellow Jackets and Black Beauties for the most part. But they often had Valium, and I liked those better. They calmed me. They calmed me so much that first hour math class seemed interesting. I'd glaze over like a feeble-eyed savant and the hour would pass before I was even aware of it having begun. You could buy three Valiums for a dollar, and for the next few years, that's where my lunch money went. I graduated high school and pretty much forgot about pills, aside from the occasional handful of Quaaludes while drinking.

I never went to college.

When I was eighteen I started seeing a shrink. That's when I turned. I could get just about anything I wanted from this guy, along with a raft of shit I didn't want, and after eight years in his care I was a walking pharmaceutical wreck. I got off all of it, after much difficulty, and swore I'd never touch anything like it again.

And for the next seven years, I didn't.

It was work related.

There was a guy, a regular, his name was Marcus. He had three kids and a wife and a house in a nice neighborhood near the bar where I worked. He was barely forty but he had a bad back, some slipped disks and an arthritic spine, and it fucked with him pain-wise and every other way, so he was on disability and trying to be a stay at home dad and a husband and a fledgling songwriter and a full blown prescription drug addict as best he could. His kids were all in school and his wife worked a lot, so he was often at the bar, scribbling in his notebooks, shooting the shit, and nursing a beer. His standard uniform was a cowboy hat, Hawaiian print shirt, khaki shorts, and a pair of mirrored sunglasses that were up on his forehead or on his face, depending on this, that, or the other thing.

"I left something special in your jar," he told me one afternoon.

The place was close to empty so I reached into the tip jar to see what he'd left. I figured it was a joint. He was generous that way. I pulled out a wadded up piece of toilet paper.

"Thanks a lot," I said, but he was already out the door.

I unfolded the toilet paper and there were four blue pills inside, tiny things, along with a wee bit of notebook paper that had the word MILK written on it.

MILK?

I took one with a glass of wine. I took a shower and fed the cats. I started to feel good. Then I started to feel great. Then I began poking around the apartment for my copy of the *Complete Guide to Prescription and Non-Prescription Drugs*, H. Winter Griffith, M.D. 1995 Edition.

Dilaudid—See NARCOTIC ANALGESICS 592

I remembered reading a biography on Lenny Bruce. He was quoted as saying that taking Dilaudid felt like a sunflower opening up in his belly. I don't know about sunflowers, but it did feel good. It made me feel like butter, loose, happy butter.

What drug does:
   Blocks pain messages to brain and spinal
   cord.
   Reduces sensitivity of brain's cough control
   center.
Time lapse before drug works:
   30 minutes.
Don't take with:
   Any other medicine without consulting your
   doctor or pharmacist.

I had another glass of wine. Then I gathered my keys and some change for the bus. The Fireballs of Freedom were playing at Satyricon that night, and I wanted to take some pictures with the new camera I had recently gotten in trade for a painting I had made years prior. Taking pictures was going to be my thing again. I needed a hobby. On the bus, I took another Dilaudid. The driver saw me do it. I raised my camera and took his picture. "Take my picture again and you'll be walking," he said.

17

The next day I dropped off my film at a one-hour photo place on Northwest Burnside. I went to the Matador to wait. I had two or three drinks while staring into space. I put a dollar into the jukebox. Looked at the bulls on the walls and the bull fighters fighting them. Took a picture. Then I went and picked up my photos and headed back to the bar to look at them. They were pretty good, but I couldn't remember taking most of them. When did I climb up onto the stage? I kept flipping through them. Some were great, shot from slightly above and directly behind the band. You could see the hair and the sweat of the band members and the twisted, blissed out faces of the crowd. I kept flipping. I came to a shot of a girl with blue hair and black lipstick posing on an unmade bed. She had her top off. I had never seen her or the bed before.

I ordered another drink. The place was dead. It was just me and the bartender and the stale afternoon air and the nicotine stained everything.

I kept staring at the girl with the blue hair and black lipstick. She had pale blue eyes that matched her hair, big pink nipples and a sexy smile. I wondered if someone else's pictures had gotten mixed in with mine. I felt uneasy, like a panic attack was coming.

An old woman walked in and sat down on the stool next to mine. She ordered a can of Hamm's. The bartender gave it to her and she paid him in dimes and nickels and pennies which she pulled one by one from a little rubber change purse. The blue haired girl was on the bar.

"Cute picture," the old woman said. "Is she your sweetie? I have a picture. Wanna see?" She had a big white rag doll looking wig tied to her head with a rope. The rope went over the top of the wig and the ends were knotted together beneath her chin.

"Sure," I said.

She pulled a photo from one of her bags and held it close to my face. I had to pull back to get it in focus. A naked brunette pulling a starlet pose in a 1950s living room.

"That's me," she said, "before I got old and ugly."

"You look like Bettie Page."

"I looked *better* than Bettie Page."

The bartender walked over and confirmed it. "It's true," he said.

"Goddamn right," she told him.

"Goddamn right," I said. "Barkeep, I'd like to buy Better Than Bettie a drink."

"I'll have a vodka soda," she told him.

Jukebox music ensued. We toasted the air, nothing in particular.

"My name is Vera," she said.

"Nice to meet you, Vera."

I tucked the blue haired girl into my pocket along with the rest of my pictures. I wondered who she was. I wondered who I was.

I knew who the woman with the wig was.

Her name was Vera, and she had once looked better than Bettie Page.

Sleep

I worked nights in a bar I couldn't stand and rarely got to bed before the birds began to chatter and the worms got gotten and people started their cars and the world shimmered outside my window in waves of carbon-monoxide and monotonous regularity. If the sun was out I'd lay there in bed and let it crawl all over me. If it was raining, I'd pull the sheets over my head and hide. Today it was sun, lots of it. Sun was always nice, if you didn't have a hangover, or a wife that rose at the crack of dawn.

I heard her footsteps in the hall, her keys rattling in her hand. She was bi-polar and had a job so high-stress it made her hair fall out. She opened the door, back from whatever it was she'd been doing. She was always up and moving half a day before I was even aware of my own existence. I could hear her moving around out there in the kitchen. It was a good sound, her walking around like that; a comforting sound.

"Baby, are you hungry? It's noon, come talk to me."

I got out of bed and walked to the kitchen.

"I brought you a Whopper," she said. "Sit down."

I sat down and unwrapped my Whopper. I lifted the bun and pulled off the pickles. Something was wrong. I couldn't put my finger on it.

"You alright?" I said.

She looked out the window. The window looked out onto a ravine where homeless people liked to camp while waiting for their lives to begin again or end. She said, "How was work last night?"

"It was a train wreck. They hired someone who's never waited tables before. They always wanna train new people on Friday nights."

"Throw them right into the fire. Maybe it's better that way."

"Not for the rest of us. Christ, you should see her tits. I've never seen tits so big. It's ridiculous." I took a bite out of my Whopper.

"Listen, we have to talk."

"Sure, what's up?"

"I'm leaving, sweetie."

"What?" I set the Whopper down.

"I'm leaving," she sobbed. "I'm sorry. I wanted to tell you sooner."

"What do you mean, you're leaving?"

"I found an apartment."

"Where?"

"It doesn't matter where."

"You're leaving?"

"It's too late. I've already signed a lease."

I didn't say anything. I couldn't speak. I couldn't move, couldn't think.

"Eat your Whopper," she said.

I collapsed in a taco bar later that evening.

I'd been out drinking all day with a couple of friends from work. They were trying to sober me up. "You need to eat," they kept telling me. But it was way too late for that. I had another beer. Then I broke, and the tears came. Then they carried me out of there.

I crawled up the stairs on my hands and knees, walls spinning, world spinning, one eye working, the other screwed shut, spinning, spinning, spun, found my keys, and eventually got the door to my apartment open—our apartment. I turned on the lights and there she was on the couch, waiting for me. I crawled towards her. I stopped. I couldn't keep my head up. I tried to focus on my hands, on the floor. I was drooling. I could see it pooling there on the hardwood, between my hands, right where my hair was hanging.

"Are you okay?"

"I don't want you to leave," I said. "I don't want to be divorced."

She helped to me to couch, put my head in her lap.

"It's going to be alright," she said. "Everything's going to be okay."

My mother used to tell me the same thing when I was a boy. "You're going to be alright. Everything's going to be okay." I always had my doubts. But what else can a mother say?

"You're a liar," I told her.

"Go to sleep," she said.

Shell

I have a sea-shell I've kept since I was a kid. Large, fake looking, pink on the inside. When I hold it to my ear I can hear my parents arguing.

Sit down, I tell her, try it.

She stands there, the sea-shell pressed to her ear.

I watch her the way I watch TV when I'm sick.

The Doors Are Closing

At age forty-eight I am only important to my cats. And Ala's horns are always poking me. Day after day I hold the pink end of a pencil to the air and erase her. "Good morning," I say, and re-draw her, sans horns, but never erase well enough. It's always time to feed the cats or brush the cats or cuddle the cats, time to change the litter box or pay the bills. I carve a smile in the mirror while shaving, bleed and go to work.

A man and a woman enter, seat themselves, touch symbols on their phones. In my mind I fire three shots. In my mind we are always falling dead like autumn leaves. Dial tones of phones when the grid goes down.

Jefe' wants to know who's winning the game.

"When I left home the house was winning, but that was a lifetime ago."

"Go Packers!" Jefe' says.

Childhood is a mountain of sugar and salt. Fruit Loops and pork rinds and Wonder Bread. I sometimes miss it. My apartment is warm. I'm always wishing I was in it, until I am. So I leave again and a kid says, "Got a cigarette?"

"Nope."

"Okay, be a faggot, then, faggot."

I board the MAX, grab a strap, hang from it, see the kid's face in the window as the train drowns his sound. He's shouting "faggot," mouthing it large so there's no mistake, as if the word were not a mountain or an ocean or a mailbox in a forest looping back to my fire escape. Blackened skins of bananas moving in the breeze. Toast that won't surrender its shape. Cheese. Neighbor kids pointing skyward, saying "See, he puts food in his tree." I eat through the faces of the people crushed around me. MAX tells us the doors are closing. A girl catches a glimpse of herself in my sunglasses, takes a selfie with her phone, holds it up for me to see.

23

I have exactly one picture of my mother, bless her heart. The picture was taken on Halloween, and she is dressed as Dracula.

This picture, hung on the wall of everywhere I live, watching over me.

Time to leave the apartment again.

Big round world on a string grid, made small and oppressive. I enter as the doors are closing, cling to a pole, city rushing by, windows stuffed with billboards.

Straight away I pull a three-top. Middle-aged man and his parents. They come every Saturday, ask for separate checks. One for the parents (gray, barely there) and one for the son (pants hiked high, socks exposed.) The son orders halibut. The parents order cod.

They eat in silence, always. Exchange no words except to order and pay. Nod *yes* or *no* to any questions asked. Always the same order, ordered in the same way. I dub them Project Independence, speculate on their story, imagine sad, impoverished scenes, project them on a wall in a prison cell on the bar TV. I wear a black apron weighed with ballpoint pens, say things like "Tartar or cocktail sauce? Fries or salad? Hi. Thank you. Goodbye."

The four of us. On display like this. Season after season.

The son drops a fork, asks for another. I hand him one, hold tight for a moment as he pulls, loosen my grip and let go.

I pull the shades on the parking lot, bite down on a piece of nicotine gum, run my *American Spirit* pitch past Jefe'.

"We're all dead Indians," he says.

At home, my cats leave their waste on the floor next to the toilet. They're saying something, but what? The litter box is clean. The water bowls are fresh, the food bowls are full. I feel homesick for a freedom that no longer exists. So do my cats, I suppose. Maybe they're ill. Maybe I'm ill, too.

A woman who lives across the street enters, tells me it's a religious holiday, and would I please remove the laundry from her dryer. I follow her out the door and into her home. Remove a load of towels. Stop the buzzing sound that drove her to me. Spiritual loophole. Non-believer takes the bullet. No one goes to hell. Or do they? Her husband hides, embarrassed, in the bedroom. He sees me see him, pulls the door closed.

Everywhere I look there's food. And the woman's nervous smile. And the husband hiding in the bedroom. She rewards me with soup and salad, bags it, sends me back into the world.

"State your faith," hollers Jefe'.

I toss him the bag as the room fills with bodies. Dinner rush. A screaming child.

Jefe' digs in. He's high, has a clean Packers shirt for every day of the year. The days are mostly the same, duplicates, like the shirts.

Mayan co-workers fry fish, do the dishes. I run in circles, taking orders, leveling years. Eight, sinking into nine, nearing eternity. Overcast and cold today, rain.

Flashbulbs freeze me in various poses. Even music locks me in place. Your face forever on the radio as I fall asleep in the backseat, going wherever it is people go in the night.

Home, I'm guessing, or through a guardrail, into a tree.

Jefe' points a remote. "What's your game plan?"

The Elephant Isn't Talking

"Tell me about this one," she said.

April was sitting on my couch, looking at one of my paintings. I was sitting next to her, looking at her legs. The painting was loose and aggressive, with a bit of black humor tossed in: a skull and a factory worker and an ATM machine and a list of actresses from the golden age of porn. Under the skull I had scrawled the word COVET in bright yellow oil stick.

"That one is a snapshot of 21st century servitude," I told her. "It's a portrait of one of my dead uncles."

"Your uncle is a bit disturbing. I like it."

"You want it?"

"No, it'd give me nightmares. But I could live with that one over there."

She pointed to one of my old ones. I was in love when I had painted it, and it showed. It was two figures, a male and a female, growing into and out of one another, their body parts all mixed together, intertwined, assimilated. It was oppressive.

"It's yours," I told her. I'd been giving away paintings to anyone who happened to drop by—older paintings, for the most part—anything that reminded me of my wife, anything that reminded me of love.

"Do you believe in God?" she asked.

"What?"

"Do you believe in God?"

"Is this a trick question?"

"No, it's just that sometimes when you look at a painting, or listen to a certain song, you get the feeling that God had something to do with it."

I put my hand on her thigh. She was wearing fishnet stockings. I walked to the kitchen and brought back two beers.

"God wants you to have a beer. Drink up."

"Don't make fun of me."

"I'm not making fun of you."

"Yes you are. You don't even believe in God, do you?"

"Well..."

"How can you be an artist and not believe in God?"

"I don't understand the connection."

"What's the point? If nothing means anything, why bother to create?"

"I don't know. I'm not even sure why I bother getting out of bed in the morning. Maybe you should ask Jean-Paul Sartre or that elephant in the Portland Zoo whose paintings sell for five thousand dollars a pop."

"I would, but Sartre's dead and the elephant isn't talking."

"God isn't talking, either."

"I know. It's hard being a seeker these days."

"A Christian with a sense of humor, I like that."

"Give me a kiss," she said.

"If nothing means anything, why bother kissing?"

"Oh, just shut up and fuck me."

I put on an old Judas Priest record.

"I love Judas Priest!" she said.

She took her skirt off. I put my face between her legs and began tearing away at the stockings with my teeth. They were well-made, the fishnet wouldn't give.

"Oh God, oh God, oh God," she moaned.

It reminded me of some graffiti I once saw spray painted on the side of a train in the Chicago subway:

Joanna sees visions of Catholic saints when she comes
I don't come at all
We never go to the movies again

I had no idea what the hell it meant, but I thought about it all the way home.

Notes Found While Rummaging Through a Drawer on a Rainy Day

1

She goes into my kitchen to make toast.
You should buy a new toaster.
Why?
This one is ugly.
So what? It still works.
Yeah, but it's ugly.
It's a toaster. I'm not driving it around. I'm not trying to pick up chicks in it.

2

The Cincinnati airport has a tiny glass-walled smoking lounge. Everyone's hair looks insane.
It stinks in here. A man in a NEVER FORGET tee talks loudly of his cousin's cancer. "It started in his colon, went to his liver then his brain." I light up, think about my colon/ liver. I already know about my brain. Another dozen smokers crowd into the already crowded enclosure. Someone passes gas. I'm up against the glass, bug-smashed, elbows in my back. It takes me the duration of one cigarette to conclude that our wars will never end and that cancer may well be preferable to the Cincinnati airport smoking lounge.

3

When I meet M's family, I become acutely aware of the tear in my jacket.
I take off my jacket and realize I am wearing a sweater with holes in each armpit.
I am asked to remove my shoes.
I am wearing black socks.
The right sock has a hole from which my heel juts.
On my heel there is a blister that makes me feel naked.

Frame

So for lack of anything better to do, or maybe to hide, she stops by and stays half the night, night after night.

Today she's early.

I'm on the couch, drinking a beer, half asleep, half watching a program on OPB. I have my feet thrown over a crate and a newspaper in my hand, the beer balancing on my belly, rising and falling with my breath, the newspaper slipping from my fingers, blue light of television sucking at my face.

Leticia doesn't say anything. Neither do I.

The apartment is crippled Americana, cramped, claustrophobic, filthy, but affords a view of two mountains I have no way of visiting. It's an apartment I pay six hundred and seven dollars a month to live and lay around in, listlessly. I think it's an alright place, as alright as any, really. Leticia doesn't think about it—it isn't her place. Leticia and I both work shitty jobs and the shitty jobs take a toll and pay next to nothing. Well, *my* job pays next to nothing. Leticia spreads her legs on a stage and the dollars come flying, pussy being a more valuable commodity than the ability to bus a table. Leticia sometimes wonders how I make it. Leticia sometimes wonders how she makes it, how anyone makes it, and why bother.

I yawn and stab the remote.

A man walks across the screen, pulling a small wagon. In the wagon sits a television: Dot pattern of a dot pattern. In the center of this second screen stands a man wearing a boxy blue suit, white dress shirt, a long red tie. The man is smiling, waving his arms in a gesture of welcome, as if to say, "Come on down, you'll like it here." I think he might be trying to sell a car. But I don't see any cars. The man appears to be standing in the center of nowhere.

I look at Leticia. "You want a beer?" I have a six pack out, on the floor, by the crate my feet are resting on. I'm pointing to the can that hasn't been opened yet. I have coffee on in the kitchen.

Leticia takes the beer, pops the tab. She walks into the kitchen and comes back with a cup of coffee. A drink in each hand, one up, one down. "It's a white trash speedball," she

29

laughs, and paces around the living room like that, raising the beer to her mouth, raising the coffee cup, arms going up and down, turning in circles, humming to herself.

I take my feet off the crate and hang them over the torn up arm of the couch. They aren't a part of me anymore. In my dreams I'm always hacking them off—or someone else is. In my dreams I'm almost always dying. Or someone else is.

Leticia stops pacing.

She flops down in a chair by the window. She looks at the mountains, drinks her beer.

"I can't stand the daytime," she says. "I hate it."

"Nights are worse," I tell her.

The man on TV, the one in the televised television, jumps up and down, waving a tiny flag, stars and bars, red, white and blue. The first man is gone. He's left his wagon sitting there. It's the 4th of July.

I get up, walk to the refrigerator and back, slowly, like a man underwater. Leticia looks at the TV. I'm thirty-six years old. In high school I ran track and won awards, but then high school passed and I got hammered by things and now I move like everybody else. That's a lie. I never ran track, never won awards. I hand Leticia another beer. I keep one for myself and set our empties on the crate. We drink the beer and don't say anything for awhile. The air is thick. From outside comes the sound of people and automobiles. Firecrackers. Half an hour passes. Nothing else comes.

"I should move out of here," I say. "Not this place, this place is okay. I mean the state, the country, the whole fucking thing."

"Where would you go?" Leticia says. She's stretched out on the floor now, shoes kicked away, hands folded at the chest.

I make a vague motion with my beer.

"I don't know," I say. "Somewhere."

"I know what you mean," she says. She's calm on the Xanax she swiped from my coffee table.

"Have you heard from Claire?"

Claire and Leticia used to dance together in one of the clubs where Leticia works. Claire moved back to L.A. to try to kick heroin at her mom's house.

"No," Leticia says, "not since that postcard."

"That was a long time ago. Want another beer?"

"Sure."

I make the trip to the refrigerator. It seems a long way to go. Leticia changes the channel and the man in the little red wagon disappears. Now a group of policemen are bashing down the door of a house in Detroit. They have axes and guns and snarling dogs and they're lining people up against a living room wall. A reporter is following the action with a microphone, talking into the camera, out of the television, at Leticia, at me, at anyone who cares to listen.

"Fucking Fox News!" Leticia says.

"It's COPS," I tell her.

"It's fucking everybody!" She laughs.

Upstairs a woman is screaming at a man who is hanging a picture incorrectly, and the man is screaming back. The hammering is bad but the voices are worse. It's the anger in the voices that's shaking the walls, I'm sure of it. Pound! Curse! Pound! Curse! Pound! Pound! Pound! I wonder what it's a picture of.

"Fucking lunatics," I say. Leticia grins. I put my head in my hands, lift it like a heavy rock and let it drop to the back of the couch, legs spilled out in front of me. I cock my arm and hurl a beer at the ceiling. It explodes over the room in a wet, glassy rain. The neighbors hang their picture.

"I think she's in trouble," Leticia says.

"I think I am too," I tell her.

"I'm serious," she says. "I'm worried about her."

"Who?"

"Claire."

"What else is new?"

"I know. But I think it's worse now."

"I like Claire."

"I don't know what happened," she says.

"What happens to anybody?" I say.

"I should fly out there. I wanna know what's going on."

"Why don't you call her mother?"

"Her mother won't let her talk to me."

There's a loud knock at the door. I get up and press my eye to the peep-hole. There's a man out there. An older man.

"Who is it?" Leticia says.

31

I hold my finger to my lips. Leticia goes quiet.

The man is wearing sunglasses. He pushes them onto his forehead. His eyes are black holes. Jaws clenched tight, staring straight ahead. I know the look. I've lost things, too. Some more important than others.

I watch him through the peep-hole.

He stands there, waiting.

I think I know what he wants. Does he even know where he is?

I open the door and let him have it.

Again we have ordinary surroundings: a wide river with a bridge of logs. A man is carefully stepping over the logs which are falling apart. The part he has crossed is already under water so he cannot turn back. The river, grey and green, appears to have a metallic surface and the sky seems to be made of lead.

Rail

I stop while passing it, knock. Maybe I just think I knock. Or think I just thought about it but really did.

The door flies open.

> Who are you?
> I'm his dad.
> Fuck off!

She slams the door. But not before I catch a glimpse of how the better half lives: votive candles and candy wrappers, bookshelf, a shoe, part of a red couch, a shadow that must be a chair.

Red hair, red lips, red couch. I'm betting the chair is red too, if it is a chair.

What kind of word is that, chair? It's the sound a train makes. Not anything you could sit on. Or is it in—on or in the chair?

Chair chair chair chair chair chair chair...

Say it a thousand times, you'll lose your mind.

Ambulance

"Okay, look desperate, like you're about to jump!"

"What?"

"Look desperate!"

I *felt* desperate. I was leaning over the railing of the Ross Island Bridge, a river of cars racing by, doing some photo work with a guy I knew from the bar. He was a corporate photographer who made his money shooting oil drilling operations around the world. He'd go to various countries, document shit for their trade rags, and return home, flush with cash. He'd been doing it for twenty years and was getting bored. Now, against the advice of his agent, he was trying his hand at stock photography. He was paying me fifteen dollars an hour to model for him. He liked my look, my look being anxious, depressed, genuinely miserable. He had me sitting in dive bars. He had me wandering the streets with my eyes to the pavement, lost in a haze. He had me loitering on the sidewalk in front of porn stores, strip clubs and whack shacks—sad sad sad.

Now he had me on the Ross Island Bridge.

"You need to look more desperate!"

"Fuck off, I'm coming down!"

I loosened my grip on the support cable I was holding and jumped off the railing and back to the bridge while passing motorists blew by well above the speed limit.

"Did you get me almost getting hit by that car?"

"Yeah, that was great!"

"Let's get out of here. I have to go to work soon."

"Where do you want me to drop you?"

"The Matador. You got that thirty bucks?"

It was slow at work that night so after getting high with my co-workers in the break room, I volunteered to go early. I was on my way back to the Matador, hoping to find a woman named Jasmine. I knew more Jasmines than a normal person would, but I knew that this particular Jasmine more or less lived at the Matador. We drank together now and then. She was lost, like me. And sad. And fun. And funny.

I was half loaded and looking for her.

I passed a guy sitting in front of the Taco Bell on Burnside and 21st.

"Hey, you got a buck?"

I gave the guy a buck, kept walking. I had just given fifty cents to a guy standing in the parking lot of the supermarket a block back. Before that, I had given five dollars to a woman who had a shopping cart full of everything she owned in front the bar to which I had recently been transferred. It was a big bar with a big staff and a crazy-making clientele consisting mostly of mainstream college aged Chad's and Joey's and the cheerleaders who adored them.

A mall punk with perfect teeth, hundred dollar shoes, and a skateboard under his arm asked me for a quarter as I waited for the walk light at 19th.

"Fuck off," I told him.

"Give me a cigarette."

"Fuck off."

He called me a fascist.

I made it to the Matador without paying any further tolls.

The guy working the door was naked save a child-sized jockstrap, testicles strangled and exposed, checking IDs—a friend of mine. He kissed me on the mouth. I pulled away before he could grab my crotch.

Jasmine was the way she usually was: hunched over the far end of the bar in animated conversation bordering upon argument with a total stranger.

I sat at the opposite end of the bar and ordered a drink. After work, it usually took me two or three drinks until the stress began to dissipate. Until then, conversation was next to impossible. I'd drink and stare into space, waiting for the alcohol to take the edge off, hoping to come to life again. People were hard to take when you were sober, and I took hundreds of them a day. Waiting on them, pouring them drinks, serving them food, listening to them talk. It had been eight months since I'd lost my glasses. I just couldn't get around to replacing them, which was okay, really. I didn't need to see clearly anymore. I didn't want to see clearly. Things were too clear to me already. I'd have gotten a job in a place more suited to me, but I didn't know how, or what

36

that place might possibly be, or if there even was a place more suited to me. I would have rallied and gotten my life together, just a bit. But I didn't know how. Knowing that nearly drove me insane sometimes.

She grabbed me from behind. I spilled my drink.

"Hello, Jasmine."

"Sorry about your drink! Good to see you!"

"Thanks."

She waved a credit card in my face. "What are you drinking?"

"I can buy my own."

"No, let me buy you a drink. I'll open a tab."

"Okay."

We were in trouble now. Once the credit card came out, money no longer seemed real. Conceptually, you were drinking for free. And the drunker you got, the freer it seemed. Jasmine had credit cards. Maybe her parents had money. She ordered us drinks.

"You already have a tab open on another card," the bartender told her.

"Do I?"

"You opened it when you came in. That guy down there is still drinking on it."

"Which guy?"

"The guy you've been talking to for the past hour."

"But I'm not even sitting there anymore!"

"You told me to put him on your tab."

"Well take him off!"

"Okay, he's off." He looked at me, then back to Jasmine. "You want me to put this guy on your tab?"

"Of course, he's my friend."

"I'm her friend," I said.

"You sure have a lot of friends, Jasmine."

"That's enough," I told him.

He wandered off to smoke a cigarette. A dozen or so people needed drinks. He leaned against the register and opened an entertainment newspaper.

"He's right," I said to Jasmine. "You shouldn't be so generous."

"You mean careless?"

37

"People take advantage."

"I've seen you blow plenty of cash in here. I've seen you buying drinks for people you don't even know."

"Yes, but when that happens I'm drunk and not thinking correctly. You do that too often, people take you for a sucker. And they're right."

"I hate talking about money. I hate thinking about money."

"I have to think about money. I'm always one paycheck away from losing my apartment."

"You worry too much."

"Someone has to worry about me."

"Sweetie, I would never let you go homeless."

"You barely know me."

"I know you well enough. I know you want another drink."

The owner came out of kitchen and water-ballooned a table of four by the jukebox. Wham! Wham! Wham! Wham! Sometimes, it was bags of water, other times, buckets. But only on certain nights. He had dog nights, too. There would be half a dozen dogs, sitting on stools at the bar. None of this was weird, but you would only know that if you were a regular, and if you were a regular you didn't care. Like the doorman's jockstrap.

I drank with Jasmine and her credit card for close to five hours. Then she started on about about 9/11.

"I have to go home now," I told her.

"Why?"

"I'm seeing double. And it's last call."

"Let's have one more. Then we can go to my place."

"Forget it, I can't even see straight."

"Here, try on my contacts." She popped her contacts out into the palm of her hand.

"It doesn't work like that, our eyes are different."

"How do you know?"

"I'm guessing."

"You're not even going to try?"

"It isn't going to help."

"Please?"

"Okay, okay!"

"Goodie!" she said. "Tilt your head back and look at the ceiling. Don't blink."

I tilted my head back and almost fell off my bar stool.

"Hold still!" she said.

"I'm trying!"

"Try harder!"

She was drunk and she had sharp fingernails. She kept poking me in the eyes, trying to force the contacts into place. I could feel them under my eyelids. They felt like fire ants. I jumped up screaming and rubbed one of them out onto the floor. The other one seemed to be lost in my left eye socket somewhere.

"GET IT OUT!" I told her. "YOU'VE BLINDED ME!"

She was laughing so hard she could barely hold onto her drink.

"I'M SERIOUS! IT'S LOST BEHIND MY EYEBALL!"

"Oh, come here, you big baby!"

She dug around in there with her fingernails until she found the thing. I sat at the bar, rubbing my eyes, tears streaming down my face.

The bartender walked over with Jasmine's tab, threw it down in front of her. She signed it. He looked at me.

"You're a dumb-ass," he laughed.

"I've already figured that out," I told him.

"Let's get out of here," Jasmine said.

"Where do you live?"

"Four blocks from here. I live in the 911 building. That's the address. Isn't that weird?"

"It wasn't weird a month ago, was it?"

"Yeah, it was weird even then. I brought these Arab guys over one night. I met them here. When we got to my building they all laughed when they saw the address. They told me not to go anywhere on 9/11. They told me to stay at home."

"Bullshit."

"It's true! After it happened, I was scared. I'm still kinda scared. I keep thinking they're going to come looking for me."

"Who?"

"I don't know—the government?"

"Why?"

"Because of what I know!"

"What do you know?"

"I don't know!"

"Did you stay in that day?"

"No, I had to go to work."

"Do you have to work tomorrow?"

"I have to be there at nine."

"Then we'd better get out of here. Where is this place anyway?"

"It's really close."

We stagger to Jasmine's car as illegal wars are waged on the lawns of distant newspapers.

I UNDERSTAND AND I WISH TO CONTINUE

Group Shot

Claustrophobic room above the drugstore coat of lead paint cracks in the ceiling in her face. A kind of holding cell for fuck ups and losers looking back on ex-wives and girlfriends. He stays in that place.

Old guy, buys us beer. The water tower, the room. His mouth is lined with lead. People get sick here, get cancer.

Hey, mister.

She gave us some.

We go to the dump, shoot bottles and cans, rats. No shoes. Me and Duane. And the guy and the girl. Georgia somewhere. That's all he told us so that's all we know.

She's mute, has a Bugs Bunny tattoo.

Sitting there sucking down beer sharing our weed with him. Jumpy. Wants to drink, needs company. The girl never laughs. Stag films. Fed there. Or whatever his name is. Nervous, likes to talk. I have a couple of uncles like that.

Put my finger on it. Here. The basement.

One of them left a darkroom took an interest in a teenager then outgrew it. Without windows. Soft-core porn and hot-rod mags, old curling photos, forgotten shoes and socks. My negatives. I print some.

"Mom" 1979 (11 x 16) $200.00 (unframed.)

It's just kids fucking around popping pills boozing it up and the funerals with the parents wailing. Windshields spattered with blood. Dad takes us there. The dump the junkyard. He looks nothing like us.

Leave for good no one cares you're a broken home. Never say what's broken about it. Long bridge. There's a sign just as you pass says ENTERING.

He isn't really a friend.

I have these people popping up all around me no good. Knew it right away. Tried to kiss her. Some pot or booze or a plan to build a boat that just might float and off we go in a big blue car wreck. Bottles and cans mostly. Sit up there and sweat an old fan turning circles watch me try to play my out of tune guitar hero. There's a window leads out onto the roof shimmy down a pipe and you're gone. Get back in the same way. Not that you can't walk in and out the front door like a real person.

Dyed black, greased back.

Shoots worms full of air to float on the lake—fishing trick at a party trying to get into his daughter's pants—diabetic— explained what he was doing and why.

I wouldn't but wanted to and couldn't so he did it for me. Kept my eyes closed. Fucking her. Pulling his hands away and laughing. Needle bouncing up and down. I couldn't watch that for long. Shoving Saturday morning cartoons into his mouth sitting next to me on the couch. Got it done once he finished. Stopped calling him an asshole. Or one of my brothers or sisters. Fed there. Nothing happened. I was kind of wishing that girl would let go. Let's do it again a bunch of the stuff. Clean out an old lady's medicine cabinet after mowing her lawn. Not hard to come by. Unzipping our pants. Jesus, wait awhile. Listened to some records I couldn't play along with. Jesus, wait awhile. Drooling like idiots.

He didn't say just and he didn't say pussy and he didn't say fake but I knew that's what he meant.

A rotating set of costumes and a chain running from his wallet to his belt loop. Next day he's a cowboy. My mascot. Wants to be like us. Normal. We joke about him behind his back.

The way they sit or stand or walk or look at you and look away. He was either gone so much or around so much I couldn't see him anymore. After that you're on your own. Trying to scare the little monsters begging candy on the porch. Some lady dressed as Dracula. Me, peering over her shoulder.

He's hiding in the library. There's a hole. I know these people. I know this place. And the AC is always on her.

Talking along the edge of it. An alpha guy gets all the girls like in vacation photos but I keep that a secret. His smile. Scary, that's what. And I want him to like me. A good kid more or less. How do people get that way?

Here. Same place I've always been.

A pit he dug in their parent's back yard that he puts the dog down and covers up with a piece of plywood piles bricks on top while screaming. Shoes and socks. His sister. Grows up to be a prison guard in Jackson after I move to the city and she comes to see me one night. That's where they'll stay for now. That place is no better than here.

They're all the same girl. Postcards with no words. Smiley faces.

I only take one and it's a group shot. Old lady's medicine

cabinet. The negative, never print it. Picking at a scab on her arm with a safety-pin and a bottle of India-ink. The one we all dream about jack off sit close to. Look both ways. Collide with her at a mall she's been committed to. She'll be there on a three hour off grounds pass supervised by her grandparents. Lose them and find me and I'll tear out the page she's looking for. Jump out and run or one of my brothers or sisters screaming and disappear while I explain things. Move to the city go kicking accuse her of fucking those guys. Just as you pass. Jail letters lost in the mail. Steal a car and point it like a gun. Cracks in the windshield the road in his face.

This is where you'll find me.

Doomsday babies, like dandelions, for as far as the I can see.

Funnies

A three panel cartoon of a Polar bear clinging to a tiny piece of ice, adrift in a sea of black oil, the sun grinning down.

Did you know that Polar bear liver contains toxic levels of vitamin A? The Inuit used to kill explorers in the Arctic by feeding them Polar bear liver.

Too much vitamin D will kill you as well.

Milk.

That's another cartoon, calling for another three panels.

I have nowhere else to be but here.

Dive

Marcus was over, chopping up tabs of Dilaudid. We were going to see a band later that evening. We were preparing ourselves for nothing special.

"This stuff has a different effect when you snort it," he said. "There's a rush. You might want to start with this small line here."

He handed me the mirror. There were six or seven lines laid out. I did the small one, looked at the ceiling, and immediately did two of the super-sized lines. Marcus made a face.

"What?"

"You already like this shit too much."

"Yeah, it's pretty good this way."

"You should play some music."

I walked over to the stereo, put on Miles Davis' In a Silent Way, turned the volume up.

"This is good," Marcus said.

"It is."

"Should we do the rest?"

"What's this band we're going to see, anyway?"

We ended up in a Chinese restaurant downtown. It was all a movie to me, colors, smoke, swirling lights, people weaving in and out and around me. I was swaying along with it all—peaceful, distant, detached—feeling good, feeling groovy, keeping my cool, wondering what kind of music we were in for. Snorting Dilaudid was okay. I was relaxed, elated. I didn't have a care in the world, and I felt no pain. It was a nice feeling. Then a one man band began to play.

It was Experimental Music.

Mix

A Portland Police Bureau Cold Case Homicide billboard was placed on the side of the building while I slept this morning. The racket woke me, the way gunshots sometimes do in the dead of night, but I didn't know the cause of it, just tossed and turned and struggled back toward sleep. I took a bag of trash out to the dumpster just now. Four giant, murdered faces staring down at me as I walked back in, names and frozen ages displayed below each frame.

Speak Up For Those Who Can't
$1,000 Reward

In a few months they'll be as familiar as Facebook friends, but I still won't know a thing about them, other than their names, and the age at which they died. A Budweiser billboard once hung in that space for what seemed like forever. An opiate addiction hotline number. An announcement for an OMSI exhibit featuring a pyramid and a forever young pharaoh's face, which was nice, despite being a death mask, but it didn't stay up there long. I liked it best when the space went unsold for half a year, and the wind and the rain tore the pasted layers of adverts away, continually exposing unrelated bits of text and image, until nothing remained but strips of colored vinyl that whipped the side of the building whenever the wind picked up. They would fall into the parking lot, and I would collect, cut up, and incorporate the scraps into whatever painting I was working on at the time. Reuse, recycle, rearrange the wreckage. It works, for awhile. But I don't paint anymore.

Run It

"Hey, it's Leticia, wake up!"

Leticia.

Here, there, now, then. Time is a train full of ghosts.

I'm on my living room floor, fully clothed, sun searing my eyes, head exploding. I rise like a cheap plastic Christ—cracked, bone white, made in Hong Kong—hobble toward phone. The answering machine is recording the incoming call. I stare at it.

"Hey, Mister, it's me!"

I approach, hesitate, back away, advance, pick up. The receiver lets out a high pitched barrage of shrieking feedback.

"Hello?"

"Hi!"

"What time is it?"

"I don't know. It's hot out."

"Where are you?"

"I'm here."

"What do you mean?"

"I'm outside your door."

"Why didn't you knock?"

"You always tell me to call before I come over."

"Right. You coming in or what?"

"I think I wanna come in."

I unlock the door and move to the couch, slump there. A heap of dead leaves approximating the shape of a man.

She walks in and dumps her giant purse onto the floor. She grabs a handful of fabric and a shoe box with a red ribbon tied around it, goes into my kitchen.

"GROSS! Your kitchen is disgusting!"

"I know."

"Really, you need to clean that up. You're going to catch something."

"I know."

She walks to the bathroom before I can warn her.

"GROOOOOSS!"

"I know! I know!"

She pokes her head back into the living room, laughing. "Your bathroom looks like a Tool video."

49

"That's good." I laugh. I open a blank-book, write it down. Dive bar graffiti. I'll scrawl it in oil stick above the urinal trough at Cal-Sport while pissing into the ice.

TOOL VIDEO

"Close your eyes," she says. "I'll be right back."

I close my eyes—hungover, two paychecks away from homelessness, close to forty, feeling it. I hear water spilling onto the floor. "What are you doing?"

"Just keep your eyes closed."

"Okay."

"I'm almost done. Fuck!"

"Done with what?"

"Wait a second!"

I hear the sound of her heels as she walks back into the living room. She stops a few feet short of the couch. I can feel her standing there. I have a hard-on.

"Okay," she says. "Open your eyes."

I do that...left eye first, then the right. She's wearing an electric yellow bikini and Clark Kent corrective lenses, all legs and eyes and long shiny hair as dark as my dreams, balancing atop an insanely tall pair of platform boots, transparent and filled with water. In the water there are four Siamese fighting fish, two per shoe, stylishly dying, at war with one another.

"Sweet God of Thunder, how many fish have to die during the making of this movie?"

"None," she says. "Cool, huh?"

"Hey, I just thought of one: *Cloning Christ for the New Rome*."

"I like it."

"It's a bumper sticker. Write it down. Let's run it."

"You write it down. Help me out of these shoes!"

I grab her around the waist, all one hundred and ten pounds of her, pick her up and out of the Rumble Fish shoes. She's a vaguely balanced five foot five again. My cats move closer, staring at the shoes, the fish inside.

"Thanks," she says. "Nice boner you poked me with."

"It was out of my hands, love."

"You're weird. How come you never try to fuck me?"

"I'm not right in the head."

"Put some music on."

She sits on the couch, crosses her legs.

I press play and Kurt Cobain screams.

"Are you into auto-erotic asphyxiation?" she asks.

"Not yet," I say.

"I like to be choked sometimes. And I like to be flogged. I like to give them, too. A flogging is a way more intimate thing than, say, giving a guy a blowjob or whatever."

"I see your point."

"Do you?"

"Sure." I look at her arms. "Do you share needles with people?"

"Not if I can help it. Sometimes I don't have a choice."

Her new shoes are standing in the middle of the room. My cats are flattened against the floor, ready to pounce. The fish are trying to kill each other while dying in day old water.

"Do something about those fish," I tell her.

"What's the matter?"

"They're dying."

"They're fine. They're swimming around, see?"

"There's something wrong with them."

"They're probably thinking the same thing about us." She laughs.

"Okay, that's it. I want those fish out of here." I walk over to the stereo and kill the music. I grab my keys, cigarettes, Paxil.

"What are you doing?"

"We're going for a walk."

"A walk, are you kidding me?"

"Yes, a walk. And the fish are coming with us."

"Where is there to walk to around here?"

"The river."

"Can we go swimming?"

"Whatever you want."

In my mind, I have an old film clip of me and Leticia at the river, taking apart her new shoes, dumping those half-dead fish into the polluted Willamette. The film is scratched. It skips, jerks forward, moves back. There are missing frames, no sound. There I am, shading my eyes against the glare coming off the water, baggy shorts, ghostly legs, eyes like pieces of

51

coal. There's Leticia, looking lovely in her yellow bikini and giant Jackie-O glasses, running in crazy zigzags along the shore, laughing and waving, the track marks on her arms overexposed, burned away by the blinding sun.

It's a short piece of film, and it runs off its spool in a matter of seconds. The screen goes black. I don't watch it much anymore.

"He's not gonna be funny. You can tell by looking at his hair."

—Face

Pop Pop Pop

I was always seeing things. When we first moved in, it was a plus-size hooker who worked the Honey Bucket in the lot next door. What I mean is, the hooker worked the street and brought her johns into the Honey Bucket to seal the deal. I didn't want to think about it, the stuff going on in there—the smells and so forth, the disease, the visuals—because I could picture it: her and those bottom feeder johns all crushed up against each other, going at it blindly over the stink hole in that inner city outhouse.

She was alright, though.

And I blushed the first time she called me nigga.

She looked up and—zoom—there I am sitting on my fire escape one night, smoking, same as most nights. Only this time she was looking because the john was looking. She said to him, "DAT nigga? FUCK dat nigga, he ain't no COP!"

I walked back into our apartment, which is a loft, which I still live in, and I said to my girl, "Hey, did you hear that? The Honey Bucket Hooker just called me nigga."

And my girl said, "So you're not a cop anymore?"

And we both laughed.

Every time we were out walking, someone would always pass us, this person or that, young or old, male or female, it didn't matter—neighborhood people, but of a certain type—they would look at me and under their breath they would say, "What's shakin', bacon?"

Then they would look at my girl's breasts, which are huge, and snigger.

That happened all the time.

She's an F cup. Of course it happened.

"Why does everyone think I'm a cop?" I'd say. "I don't look anything like a cop. What the fuck?"

One day my girl said, "I know what it is. It's the fire escape. It's you sitting out on the fire escape all the time smoking your stupid cigarettes. You're up there looking down on everybody."

"Are you kidding me?"

"That's it, right there."

"I'm just smoking."

"It looks like you're doing surveillance, dummy. They think you're a cop."

"Undercover?"

"Duh," she said.

And I laughed and she laughed.

Because that's the way our relationship was.

I didn't have a mustache or wear mirrored sunglasses so I thought it was kind of paranoid on their end. I didn't even wear my *prescription glasses* much. I couldn't see too well out there, except for the Honey Bucket Hooker. The Honey Bucket was right at the edge of the parking lot, up against the fence facing the lot next door, where a house was being taken apart and hauled away. But I could only sort of see her. Her big blurry shape and hot pink stretch pants. Blurry red lipstick on her face. Her big eyes.

But really, I couldn't see a thing. Not clearly. Certainly nothing that would have helped or hurt in court, or gotten anyone fingered in a line-up. There were dealers out there though, money changing hands.

I didn't sweat the Honey Bucket gal. We had a country respect, but I'd always cut my smoke short whenever I saw her. I didn't want to embarrass her; either one of us. Well, not always. Sometimes I just wanted to stay out there chain smoking cigarettes—to hell with her and whatever embarrassment there was between us—and just think about the messed-up world, or wonder about my life, or try not to think about any of it, just dream.

I never felt quite at ease in that loft—this loft—back then.

I felt like a visitor, almost. I couldn't sit still unless I was smoking.

But I wasn't allowed to smoke in here.

My girl wouldn't have it.

She wasn't a smoker, that's for sure. She didn't drink much either, or do many drugs, or eat junk food at all, and never any meat except fish, because fish aren't mammals and don't give a rat's ass about their eggs once they lay them.

She could take it or leave it, no matter what it was.

Mostly she left it.

So I didn't smoke in here. I smoked on the fire escape.

It isn't even a fire escape though, because there's no ladder going to the ground. It's just a wrought iron platform from the '40s with a cage-like rail run around it, jutting out weird from the side of the building—a balcony, of sorts.

I used to wonder what happened to the ladder.

Then I'd think of the fence and the gate you buzzed to get your car into the parking lot, and the fact that each unit had an alarm system with a motion detector and a panic button, and it made sense.

Everybody's crazy now.

Panic button? I panicked just looking at the control panel it was on—too complicated, too easy to press the wrong everything—so we disabled it.

The gizmo you had to use to get into the parking lot was bad enough.

Not that I had a car to park.

My girl did, though: a 1980 Mercedes.

It was gold and glittered in the sun on the days it wasn't raining.

I was afraid to drive it, but I was often a passenger. We'd go in and out the gate and all around together. It was my job to press the gizmo that made the gate open.

I wasn't very good at it.

There was something wrong with me, or maybe the gizmo, or both.

I'd point the thing backwards, or at the sky, or my shoe, or whatever.

Or I'd forget to do it altogether—just sit there in the passenger seat, gizmo in my lap, staring at the gate, cars honking. I'd be a million miles away.

I'd get yelled at.

One day the landlady sent all the tenants new gizmos, saying the old ones were defective, and I said, "I told you so."

And my girl said, "Stop calling it a gizmo!"

This building was once a telephone exchange, a place where people patched your calls through to other people—and vice-versa—by plugging and unplugging jacks or throwing switches or something. That's why they called it the Telephone

Exchange. Tack "Lofts" onto the name, raise the rent, and here come the white folks, right?

Well, not right away. Not all at once.

I'm glad my loft has the vestigial fire escape, not one of the others. It's the reason I agreed to move in. My girl found and fell in love with the place—there's that. But even so, if it hadn't been for that piece of iron to smoke on, I would've said, "Let's look for something else, love."

I was always out there smoking and she was always inside, wondering when I was going to come back in, or was I going to stay out there forever, or what? Because I was a smoker and she wasn't, and that's the way it was: me out there, her inside.

And my girl finally shouting: WHAT THE HELL IS WRONG WITH YOU?

I'd come in and laugh and say, "Got room for one more?"

And she would laugh and say, "Glad you're back."

I'd say, "Me, too. It's crazy out there."

And I would say, "I love you, Face."

That was my nickname for her. I was always saying it, calling out to her like that:

"Face..."

"Hey, Face..."

"I love you, Face..."

Face this. *Face* that.

Drawing out the A and putting a little whistle on the C:

Fayyyyssss...like so.

And you know what she called me? Pants. That's what she called me.

"Hi, Pants."

"Hi, Face."

"Come to bed, Pants."

"Okay, Face. I'm coming."

"Hurry up."

"I love you."

"I love you too, Pants."

Sometimes she put the word 'Fancy' in front of 'Pants,' and that always made me laugh and laugh and laugh.

"What are you doing out there, Fancy Pants?"

Ahahahaha...

"Fayyyyssss! I miss you!"

57

"I'm right here, Fancy Pants!"

She was young and sang in a band and liked to make her hair big for shows. Some nights the cops would roll alongside her in their cars, asking questions as she walked home from the train—tiny cowboy hat in her hair, toy pistols in a holster on her hips.

It wasn't all funny, though. Not everything.

One night I got off work and went to see a show and stayed out late and came home to find the street cordoned off by cop cars, yellow tape all over the place, red and blue and white lights flashing, and right in front of our building, right there at the gate, was a dead kid.

I could see his body from the bus stop. As I got closer, I saw blood pouring from his head. Right above the kid's head was the mailbox, and the names of all the people who lived in the building. My name. Her name.

And I thought: "This isn't a very safe place, is it?"

But really, compared to most cities, Portland is peaceful, and this neighborhood...it costs a lot more to live here now, but it was pretty safe, even then.

But that kid got shot—POW—in the head, 20 yards from our bed. That made me think. The newspaper said he was 14 and it was a gang thing, and that made me think, too.

And then I forgot about it, mostly. We would sometimes hear gunshots, but we never saw any more bodies. Those sounds just blended in with the freeway noise, and with the sirens, ice cream trucks, garbage, people leaving bars, busses coming and going, whack jobs screaming from the overpass...

You never knew if it was a car backfiring or a firecracker or what, because sometimes it was and sometimes it wasn't.

If the glass door that led out onto the fire escape was closed and all the windows were shut—and if you had the TV on or music playing—those sounds barely registered. It was just white noise, like something you'd hear in a seashell. A few POPS and BANGS every so often, almost always at night:

POP!
POP! POP! POP!

Silence...

BANG!
POP! POP!
POP!

"Why so jumpy? It's just a car muffler, jeez."
"Oh, it sounded like...okay."

Three months later:

POP! POP! POP! POP!
BANG!
POP!

Snore...

The absence of a ladder allowed us no escape in the event of a fire.

We couldn't get down, but nobody could get up, either. We were untouchable. Unless there was a fire, in which case we were fucked if it was the stairwell that was in flames. I'm still fucked, if that's the case.

I've been here so long there's actually a tree I've watched grow, year after year, without really knowing, and now it's almost big enough to get a grip on and get to the ground without killing myself on the razor-wire surrounding the parking lot.

That's progress.

But I still don't have a car.

Another thing that wasn't funny was taking the train from North Portland to downtown every day. And then, once I got there, having to wait for a bus to take me to John's Landing, where I work in a fish house, tending bar. It took me an hour and a half, with the layover and all the waiting. The busses never ran on time. They were either early or way late. The trains would break down, or there'd be a car stuck on the tracks and some drunk person behind the wheel screaming, "Oh shit!" so you'd miss your connection downtown.

You'd be stuck there waiting, and waiting, and waiting.

I would see some funny shit. Annoying shit, too, like people talking non-stop on their cell phones REALLY LOUD about horrific personal stuff, or just plain boring stuff, or people begging change and everybody pretending they didn't exist, the way the scrolling ads and surveillance cameras everywhere didn't exist.

I'd pretend, too, most of the time.

There was a lot not to see out there.

It's worse now.

But some of it was laugh-out-loud, still is.

Middle-aged people in florescent superhero tights, on their bikes—they're way up the list—tourists waiting in long lines for donuts, Greenpeace people shoving clipboards at you, Save the Children people, Animal Rights people.

And everywhere, people taking pictures of themselves, posting who, what and where, and clicking "I like this."

There was this one guy I would see all the time on the bus mall. He looked pretty normal from a distance: blue jeans and a tucked-in, white collared work shirt, belt cinched tight, kind of skinny, a clipboard in his hand. Always that same outfit, always with a clipboard and a pen—many pens. I figured he was working for the city, for Tri-Met or DEQ or something, maybe a planning committee, a livability study of this one particular spot downtown. He'd be crouched there on the sidewalk every day, writing shit down, all intent and focused, just writing away, recording information, very serious about it, like it was life or death, this thing he was doing. Important business, so important you wouldn't know anything about it, being a civilian and whatnot. You'd have no idea. *La la la, move along you clueless private sector people...*

And you just figured he was working.

But when you got up close, when you passed him and looked over his shoulder, you could see he had pages and pages of numbers written down, on his clipboard, and in yellow legal pads spread out in small piles all around him— IMPORTANT BUSINESS PAPERS—and the handwriting was all wrong somehow, really strangled and strange. Then you noticed his face, all the worry-lines there, and you noticed his hair, matted and shot through with gray, pasted to his forehead like fingers, with his hands trembling above the clipboard, and how frantic he was not to miss anything.

I made a point of peeking over his shoulder every day.

I finally figured out it was the busses he was recording—arrival and departure times for all the busses, trains, streetcars.

That's what those numbers were: lines, times...

One day I saw him look really quickly into the sky, then back to earth so he wouldn't miss any busses or trains arriving or departing or just zooming by not even bothering to pick people up—and there was a plane up there, way up there, real tiny, with a white tail trailing behind it, and two buses rolling towards us, and a train on the way.

And I thought: "Don't."

And I thought: "You poor bastard, what have your demons done to you?"

Then I stepped around him, the way you step around broken glass or someone with facial tattoos.

I don't know, though. About anything, really.

I have long hair and I wear what some would consider semi-ridiculous clothes. You know: skinny jeans—blue or black or gray—and black t-shirts, dress shirts with big collars, hats, a studded brown leather wrist band, Beatle boots...that kind of thing.

I've looked this way since I was 17.

But I'm an old guy now. And people think, "Well, he must be a band guy. What else could he be, walking around looking like that at his age? What kind of job could he have?"

Portland is full of musicians. There are a thousand bands here—no exaggeration—and some famous ones, too. So I'm not unusual-looking at all, aside from the fact that I don't have tattoos, because I'm not from that generation. My generation had band tees and shaggy hair, trucker wallets, Kiss. And besides, almost everyone here is covered with tattoos, even people who work in offices and cubicles or at the bank, because this is Portland and Portland is like that: full of circus freaks.

It's almost the norm.

So even if I had tattoos crawling up my neck, what would that say about me?

They say Portland is weird and that we should keep it that

61

way, but it's about as weird as a loaf of Wonder Bread, which is kind of weird, I guess, because what the hell is Wonder Bread anyway? It's white, for one thing, and stripped of all nutritional value.

It isn't even bread. It's filler, just...nothing.

And most of those musicians do the same thing I do for a living. They tend bar, they wait tables, they stand in doorways checking IDs.

But people always think I'm a Band Guy.

Maybe it's because a lot of my friends are, and I'm always walking into clubs without paying, and walking down the street without my glasses on and not seeing people's faces too clearly, or not waving hello when they wave hello or whatever, and they think I'm arrogant and aloof when really I'm just half-blind and vain, because I hate wearing my glasses. They hurt my nose and the spot behind my ears.

I'm a little precious, too. I mean, look at my pointy shoes with the buckles.

"Are you wearing a *blouse*, dude?"

"And what's up with the cowboy shirt and the fringed vest, Roger Daltrey?"

So, yeah, I get it.

But I'm almost serious: Everybody looks like they're in a band here—except for a lot of the people actually in bands. They look more like lit majors, mechanics, or zine-makers. My point is, just by looking at them, you can't really tell what the hell a lot of people are anymore.

A strange girl once said to me: "Maybe you're a vampire, and this fire escape is a perch, and this loft you live in is your lair."

"You're saying I hide from people."

"I'm saying maybe you're a vampire."

The girl watched a lot of TV. And she was a little too fascinated by the giant neon cross that hangs in the sky after the moon comes up over my fire escape.

The cross sits atop a church up the road, almost invisible during the day, and the name on the sign out front reads: *God's International Church of the Sovereign Individual*.

Which really does sound like something you'd see on TV.

It takes an alien to get that channel.

She even looked like one.
Remember rabbit ears? She had a pair of those.
"It's a crow's nest," I told her.
"Ship in a bottle," she said.

So listen.

I was with my ex-wife in a Hollywood Video one day. She lives down in NW Portland, just off Burnside. I used to like to drink in a certain dark bar there that had pictures of bulls and matadors everywhere, and we ran into each other on the street—in sunlight, no less. I hadn't seen her in ages and we were kind of catching up. She was looking for a movie to watch later that night—by herself I assumed—and I imagined her lonely, because she has this little flipper arm, like a baby's arm, and it spooks a lot of guys, but it never spooked me. In fact, I didn't even notice until the morning after we first slept together, which was the night we met. So we went into the video store. I told her that she should meet my girlfriend, meaning Face, because we had just moved in together and I had just started calling her that, and my ex-wife said that would be great, and how that kind of thing was healthy—important, even. And right when she said that, this crazy-looking young Goth girl walked up—all sunken eyes and pale and plump, but kind of cute and blushing—and she said, "Hey, I don't mean to bother you, but weren't you in a band back in the '80s?" And my ex-wife busted out laughing. She laughed so hard she knocked a huge display of movies over—fell right into it—and it was that movie, *The Truman Show*. So the video kid came over and we kind of slinked away, feeling like fuck ups, with Goth girl trailing behind and my ex-wife still laughing. The Goth girl's ears turned red and she told me her name is a city in France and I am "that guy" and I was in "that metal band," and what was my name? I felt like an ass, because I didn't look like a guy from an '80s metal band at all. Maybe a '70s band, or a '60s band—rock or new mod or something, maybe really early metal, before metal was called metal, or early punk, like the Stooges maybe—but a guy from an '80s band? No way! I didn't have big hair, for one thing (long, yes; black, yes), nor did I wear spandex or make-up or any of that.

So I just said, "No, you got the wrong guy."

My ex-wife kept shrieking with laughter, like it was the funniest thing EVER.

Then I started to feel really awkward, because the Goth girl was looking at me and her eyes were full of tears. She kept looking at me, and then looking at my ex-wife who just kept LAUGHING AND LAUGHING AND LAUGHING— back and forth like that—and then the Goth girl started CRYING—really crying, I mean SOBBING—her eyeliner running and make up getting all fucked up and ugly...

My ex-wife stopped laughing. Then she was HUGGING the Goth girl, trying to comfort her. I was just standing there, mortified, feeling like a criminal even though I hadn't done anything wrong.

My ex-wife was giving me this look that said: *Why don't you DO something about this?*

So I said to the Goth girl, "Hey, she's not laughing at you. She's laughing at me."

She looked even more embarrassed and confused, so I said, "Where did you get those shoes? They're cool."

And Goth girl smiled this tiny smile.

"I dig your hair, too," I said.

And now she was REALLY smiling. She dug into her purse, pulled out a pen and a scrap of paper, wrote down her phone number, handed it to me. "Here you go, '80s goth metal guy," she said. "Call me!"

My ex-wife didn't laugh this time.

She held it in until we got outside, and then she let it rip: *AHAHAHAHAHAHAH!*

But I didn't think it was funny.

I remembered how she had told me one morning, back when we were still married, "We need to talk," then told me she was leaving. And how she did that, and how hurt and messed up I was for years afterward; how I dyed my hair black and started drinking more, and doing drugs, and sleeping with women whose names I couldn't remember, or sometimes could but only when they had fake dancer names and track marks, and how every time someone laughed when I was walking down the street, or in the grocery store, or at work or anywhere, really—well, I was pretty sure they were laughing at *me*, even though I couldn't see them sometimes, and had no idea where the laughter was coming from.

I'm pretty sure I still have Goth Girl's number.

I think I hid it under a mess of papers in a drawer in my desk, for posterity.

I've had a cell phone for 13 months now. Before that, I had a landline, but I was rarely home, and when I was, I was out on my fire escape, or sleeping, or ignoring the phone ringing.

I would let the answering machine get it.

I wouldn't check my messages for days, weeks sometimes, so almost every message was moot, past-tense.

"Hey, buddy, we're at East End. Get your ass down here!"

"Yo, I'm in front of your building. Buzz me up!"

"Hi, sweetie, I'm going to be working late tonight. You should meet me here when we close. We'll have some drinks and go home and watch *Big Love*."

"Hi, honey, it's just your mom. Your uncle Jim died last week. The funeral was yesterday. Happy birthday! Love you!"

I felt pretty powerless, not having a cell phone. Face was always harping on me about it, but I kept putting off getting one. I hated cell phones.

The way people are constantly clutching them, checking messages, texting, talking to you, then to some other person, texting, reading text, picking up the conversation again... always in two places at once, or in another place altogether. But never where they are, or really with whomever they're with. I'm here, but I'm also there, in this other place, with these other people.

I saw people when I saw them.

I was always out, and I'd run into them, and that's when we'd talk, do things, drink. I'd do many things. But even so, even though I was always out, it was hit or miss. I'd miss things. Lots of things. I kept missing people, connections, events, gatherings...even when we had made plans, because plans change quickly when everybody has a phone in their pocket.

"Dude, you missed it! We went over to the Odditorium, Zia got naked and everyone sang."

"Yo, I bet you feel like shit today. Do you remember losing

65

that girl's contact in your eye socket last night?"

"Hey, don't bother coming in to work tonight. I know I said I couldn't cover your shift, but now I can and I really need the money, so go see that show."

"Hello, this is Providence Medical. If we don't hear back from you today, we'll go ahead and cancel your..."

"Hey moron, where are you? Sean Penn is here! We're in the green room at Dante's. Jamie hooked him up with an 8 ball and he's not sharing. It's freaky! I've never seen anything like it!"

"Hi, honey, it's just your mom again. Your brother's in Portland; he just got off the plane. He's lost and he's looking for you."

And I'd be at a bar a block away, by myself, smoking, hiding in public, so good at it now that I was almost invisible, sipping whiskey and reading the newspaper while all this stuff was happening. So many things happening, happening, happening...

And if I wasn't in a bar, I was on the fire escape.

Rain or shine, wind, snow, I was one with the elements.

I was a compound.

Smoke, that's what I was.

And it went on like that, years and years...just like that.

Then they banned smoking in bars and I spent even more time on the fire escape.

One day I went to the bar where my girlfriend worked.

I stopped in on a whim, unannounced, had a coffee and a sandwich, and I said, "Hey, Face, can I use your phone for a sec? I need to call my brother."

I didn't have my own at the time.

Face said, "Sure," and handed me her phone. I had bought it for her for Christmas or her birthday or something. She'd really wanted one, and I didn't want one, so what the hell. I stepped outside and as I was touching the screen—tap tap tap—dialing my brother, a text popped up: *Hi babe. I missed the 14 bus and I'm running late. Can't wait to see you. Love,* _____.

And my heart fell from the sky.

I went back inside, gave her the phone and said, "Thank you, Face."

And I couldn't help myself. I couldn't NOT say it, couldn't NOT ask...

"So, what are you doing when you get off tonight?"

"Oh, I'm just gonna have a drink here and then go home, I think."

I could feel the anger tearing through me, right behind the hurt, like my heart had become a hand grenade, but I knew I'd had it coming. It was exactly what I'd been asking for, even if I hadn't known it until the moment I saw that text.

I left and caught a bus to work.

When I got home, she wasn't there.

I broke some things I couldn't fix, and some I could.

All at once, I wanted to be closer to her. So close that when I looked into the mirror, I saw three faces.

The next day, I was looking at people's cell phones almost frantically, wondering which one to buy. I didn't know where to begin. I went to a phone store and the sales guy said, "This is what you need."

So I have one now, and I sort of hate it and sort of don't.

I called Face at work...

"Oh, good, you got a phone," she said.

Then she asked what kind of bread I wanted.

I heard someone say, "What are my choices?"

"Sourdough, whole wheat, or rye," she said. "What color are my eyes?"

She was talking to me.

Soon after I began living with Face, and soon after my run-in with Goth Girl, I cut off all my hair and an almost perfect thing happened—if perfect means surprising, and surprising means you cough your guts up over it.

I was standing dead drunk in front of our building one night, fumbling like a monkey for my keys, dropping them, getting down on my hands and knees, feeling around, getting up, falling.

So I lay there for a minute, on the sidewalk.

Just a minute, that was the plan.

And the Honey Bucket Hooker marched by, bursting from her spandex, and said, "Oh shit, Samson, you cut off your hair! You still ain't figured it out yet? You lost all your superpowers!"

Samson.

I laughed like a lunatic, at that.

I got up and had to squint to see our names on the mailbox. I kept reaching, trying to press the intercom button on the gate.

It took a long time.

The Honey Bucket Hooker kept laughing.

I pressed really hard.

It made a sound up there, where my girl was, then another sound, down where I was.

Spam Summary

Safe & Supervised Drug Rehab Center
A healthier life awaits with alcohol rehab
Buy burial insurance online
Will you march?

Remember This

I helped her move out. The bed, the dresser, the couch, the kitchen table, the chairs, the pots and pans and silverware, the cups, the plates, the bowls, the towels and bath soaps, the lamps, the knick-knacks, the toolbox, the jumper-cables. I helped her pack all that shit. Then I helped her move it into her new place. I didn't care about the stuff. What I wanted was her. But what I wanted was leaving, right along with the stuff.

We had everything boxed and ready to go when she got a call letting her know that her apartment wouldn't be ready for another two weeks. So for the next two weeks we lived among the boxes, all of them stacked and labeled, her sleeping on one side of the bed, myself sleeping on the other side, trying not to intersect too much. Occasionally, in a half-sleep, I'd find myself with my arms wrapped around her. She'd wake, leap from the bed and say, *"What are you doing?"*

The two weeks passed. No calls from her new apartment manager this time, no last minute stay of execution. I began drinking straight away that morning, while helping her and three of her girlfriends load the U-Haul. They were wondering what the fuck I was doing there participating in her departure. She's my wife, I wanted to tell them, this is *my* fucking life, what are *you* people doing here? But I was too shell-shocked to articulate anything I was feeling. I helped load the U-Haul and discreetly choked back any sign of emotional tailspin while running back and forth to the refrigerator for beer. I kept stealing glances at her, knowing that I would never see her that way again, still married to me, still stirring the air in our apartment, the smell of her perfume cutting through the cat-piss and cigarette smoke.

As we were humping everything down the stairs and out of the building, our neighbor from across the hall was trying to get himself and six of his half-drunk friends dressed for a wedding—*his* wedding. They all were crowded there in the hallway, shuffling their feet, pulling at their cheap rented tuxedos, drinking beer.

"Hey, man, I'm getting married today!" He had a big shit-eating grin on his face. I was dragging the box-spring portion of the bed I would no longer be sleeping on down the stairs.

"Congratulations," I told him.

We pulled up to the place where she'd be living, at the foot of the West Hills, the area where it began getting rich. The higher up the hill you went, the richer you had to be.

I need to remember, I thought. I need to remember this building, this number on the door, and how we got here.

It was a nice place, hardwood floors and a working dumbwaiter that went down to the laundry room. It was one of those historic buildings, protected by city law. The rents were steep and you couldn't change the seat on the toilet without contacting the proper authorities.

We lugged in the last of the boxes, tired, sweating, trying to ignore the elephant in the room. Tina ordered take-out and handed everyone beverages, beer, wine, or soda pop. I took the beer.

"This is a nice place," I told her.

"Yeah," she said.

"What's the bedroom look like?"

We walked to the bedroom.

"It's pretty small," she said.

"It's a nice bedroom," I told her.

She gave me a hug. I hugged her back and held it way too long. I didn't want to let go. I wanted to die and for death to be this: she and I standing in that empty room, our arms locked around one another, forever.

"I'm sorry," she said.

"I'm sorry, too."

"Are you going to be okay?" she said.

"I hope so."

Back in the living room, one of her friends was shoving furniture around, playing house. The friend flopped down on the couch, happy and relaxed. I hated her.

"This place is going to be great," she said. "You're single again. Look out Portland!"

My wife pretended not to hear her. I didn't pretend.

That was when she figured it was time to give me a lift back to the old place, home—my place, whatever the hell it was now. As we were getting into the car, a guy poked his head out the window of the apartment next door.

"Hey," he said, "are you two moving in? Do you need a bed?"

"Is that a joke" I asked.

My wife nudged me with her elbow.

"Yeah," I said, "I guess I do need a bed."

"Well, I have a bed I need to get rid of."

I got out of the car and went in and had a look at it. The guy's apartment was all but empty, save the bed and a few boxes. He was one of those impossibly good looking Euro-guys. I was half in the bag, wearing jeans and the shirt top of my torn up plaid pajamas.

"I'm moving out," he said. "My girlfriend and I are getting married."

This can't be happening, I thought.

He told me he had just graduated from med-school and that he'd hardly ever slept in the bed because he was always at the hospital or his girlfriend's place. "Med-students don't sleep much," he said.

"We're characters in a bad movie," I told him. "I'm a bartender."

"Right...So do you want the bed or what?"

"How much?"

"Seventy-five bucks. That's a steal, it's practically brand new."

"I'll take it."

He helped me break it down and load it into my wife's grey Oldsmobile station wagon.

As we were pulling away, she noticed the wheels.

"What are those all about?"

"It's a hospital bed. The guy just finished med-school. He probably got a deal on it."

"Is he moving in or out?"

"Out, he's getting married. Why?"

"That is so weird."

"I told him we were characters in a bad movie."

"That's mean," she said.

"He'll get over it," I told her.

She drove me home.

"I love you," I said.

"I love you too," she said.

I stood there and watched her drive away.

I had a bed and two cats, and all the time in the world to miss her.

Status

For weeks now, I've been watching a guy I used to see in the bars go through the first stages of homelessness on Facebook, meaning I read his updates and the comments people make on them. I'm a passive spectator. An appalled voyeur. A dead eye. He's on the street, he's angry, he's scared. I keep thinking how harsh some of the comments are. I keep wondering where his friends are. I watch him the way I watch the world burn on the bar TV.

Walls

I'd been sleeping in the living room since the split. I put my bed out there. The bedroom was now a place to store paintings. On the wall above the bed I'd taped up all the photos I had of her. Wife at the beach. Wife on the mountain. Wife in the rain. Wife on an El platform in Chicago. Wife in the kitchen with a can of RAID. Wife throwing an unopened can of marinara sauce at a fire in the bedroom. Wife jamming an Easter egg into her mouth at the age of five. It looked like a shrine and it frightened me in my more objective moments. At other times it was comforting. Mostly, it made me sad. I made some paintings of her, and hung those up, too. The Church of Wife. My friends thought I was bonkers, but I rarely had friends over anymore. The people who stopped by were strangers, for the most part. Co-workers, people I'd meet in bars at last call. They didn't care what I had hanging on my walls. I liked that about them.

Toxic Scott and the Nurse Are Sitting on My Couch, Drinking Beer

I scratch my head. "How do like the couch?" I'm sitting on my unmade bed. My cats are staring at us. I say, "Hi, babies!"

"It's comfortable," Scott says.

"It's leather," I tell him.

"White leather," the nurse says. "It's straight out of the eighties."

"I got it for free."

"Nice coffee table," she says. "You should maybe clean it off, though."

"You're right," I say.

"Those photos on your wall, that's fucked up," Scott says.

"Maybe," I say.

"Be nice, Scott," the nurse says.

"Yeah," I say, "be nice, Scott."

"She's pretty," the nurse says.

"She's my wife," I say.

"Oh, Christ, let's get out of here," Scott says.

"My name is Heather," the nurse says. "Scott has no manners."

"Sorry," Scott says. "I should have introduced you."

"Nice to meet you, Heather," I say.

"It's nice to meet you, too." Heather says. "I was married once."

"You were?" I say.

"I was married for twelve years," she says.

"Ouch," I say.

Scott clears his throat.

Heather tears up.

"Oh, Christ." Scott says.

We get out of there and go to a bar.

It's karaoke night at Suki's.

I don't sing anything, never do.

La dee da.

Debt

So I go home with a woman whose name I can't remember. We were drunk. She was a bad drunk, not very good at it. I was an enthusiast in free fall. She was all come in, get out, yes, no, stop, go, so I thought it best to leave but she blocked the door.

"Stay," she said.

I took off my coat.

"Leave," she said.

"Okay."

"Don't go," she said.

"I'm leaving," I told her.

"Then go."

"You seem angry."

"I'm not angry."

"Punch me in the face."

"Fuck off."

"Go ahead, let it out."

She broke my nose. I put my face in my hands and sobbed out the grief of who knows how many years.

"Oh my God, I'm sorry!" she said. "Let me get you a towel."

"Do you have a gun?"

"I think so."

"Go get it," I told her, instantly terrified.

She disappeared into the bedroom. I could hear her digging around in there. I wondered if she was crazy. I wondered if I was crazy. I took a look at the place, trailing blood as I walked around. It was jammed full of cardboard boxes, labeled in block letters with a black Sharpie, covered in dust, waiting. Waiting for what?

SILVERWARE. CUPS. GLASSES. PLATES/ BOWLS. SPICES. VHS TAPES. KNICK-KNACKS. CHRISTMAS STUFF. CD'S. IMPORTANT PAPERS.

There were books laying around, mostly on the couch. Books on depression, obsessive-compulsive disorder, bulimia, anorexia. The couch was the sole piece of furniture. One of the titles jumped out at me: *Adult Children of Alcoholics*. I saw that book everywhere but had never read it. I knew all about anorexia because I had it. Used to have it. Well, you know.

"Are you there?" I said.

She came back into the kitchen. "I can't find it," she said. She wet a towel. "Hold this on your nose. Pinch it. Fuck, you got blood everywhere!"

"What time is it?"

"Three-thirty."

"I have to be to work at eight."

"It's too late to catch a bus."

"I'll walk."

"Don't be crazy," she said.

"Stay here," she said.

"Don't be crazy," I told her.

I was standing at a bus stop a block from her apartment as the sun was coming up, in the suburbs somewhere, along with half a dozen businessmen who had suits and ties and jobs to go to downtown, people with wives, children, mortgages to pay. I felt sick and had dried blood all down the front of my lime green satin shirt. The men kept trying not to look at me.

The bus came and we all paid and piled aboard. I had the correct change. Exact, as always. This was my life. I was good at this sort of thing.

"Rise and shine!" the driver said.

You Are Here

My downstairs neighbor claims to be a ninja—"a real one." I see him outside on occasion, smoking a cigarette, in full ninja gear. He'll walk around the grounds, get in his girlfriend's car, and drive off to who knows where, dressed like that.

He also shoots his compound bow in the parking lot late at night. He'll set up a padded target and shoot arrows from one end of the lot to the other—thwack, thwack, thwack—safety goggles on, a bottle in his back pocket. He doesn't do it often. But how often is too often, to be drunk, after midnight, shooting a compound bow in the parking lot?

A few months ago, the woman he lives with told another neighbor of mine, "If you see _____, don't let him in the gate. He's a sociopath."

Apparently, the woman and her ninja had a falling out, and he was banished for a brief period. I hadn't noticed his absence. He's only on my radar when he's being weird, or irritating; shooting his arrows, or dressed as a ninja. I could say the same about anyone in the building.

The woman has since married him, my neighbor tells me.

"Maybe they'll buy a house," I say.

"I don't think he works," my neighbor says.

"What does she do?"

"I have no idea."

"What do you do?"

"What do you do?"

I tell her I'm a disgraced starship captain, currently employed in food and beverage.

"Have you met the people in the unit by the laundry room yet?" she asks.

"Oh, god, the Renaissance couple?"

"The Wizard and his child-bride moved out ages ago, honey."

"Really?"

"Yes, and the new people are total freaks."

DNA

She's a cum vampire.
What are you talking about?
The chick across the hall.
E3, the new girl?
Yeah, every night for a month now she knocks on my door, sucks me off and leaves.
Bullshit.
She says it helps her sleep, that she can't sleep unless she swallows my load.
That's kind of sick.
I know but.
Your load or anybody's load?
I think just mine.
It's in our DNA.
What is?
To think that way.

Que Sera Sera

I went to an appearance Nina Hartley made at Fantasy Adult Video and asked her to sign a copy of the *Boogie Nights* soundtrack as part of a wedding present for a friend. He wasn't into porn, per se. The present was an excuse to have Nina Hartley sit on my lap and pay ten dollars to have a Polaroid taken. I was a teenager during the late 70's and early 80's. This was a woman whose movies I'd spent my formative years jerking off to and feeling shameful about. Nina Hartley loomed large in my sexual mythology. Maybe a small, stunted part of me was still stuck in that place, hunkered down in front of the family TV at 3 a.m., watching Nina Hartley riding John Holmes on my mom's boyfriend's Beta-Max machine, adolescent dick in hand, hoping no one would wake up and find me like that—paranoid, guilt-ridden, excited, watching the movie, watching my back, feeling freakish, stopping, starting, listening for footsteps in the hall, a doorknob turning, a cough. Nina Hartley moaning. Nina Hartley with that massive thing in her mouth. Nina Hartley bending over and showing acres of ass. My heart pounding in my throat, excited, dizzy, coming on the carpet like a halfwit dog—*Oh God did mom just get out of bed to use the bathroom?* Wedding present for a friend, check.

"He'll get a kick out of it," I told my wife.

"I think we know who's going to get a kick out of it," she said.

"I'll be back in an hour," I told her.

I brought along one of my paintings to give to Nina. It was a nude.

"Wow, she looks just like me!" Nina said.

"I know. It's funny, isn't it?"

"I love it!" She waved her P.R. guy over. "This is my new friend. He made me this painting. Take our picture." I was nervous. Nina showed me where to put my hands.

He took a picture of us holding up the painting of the naked lady, grinning, like idiots.

"I'm going to put that on my website," she said.

I didn't have a computer. I didn't really know what a

website was. "Is it true that you were a nurse before you got into porn?"

"I was a nursing *student*. Porn was how I put myself through school. But porn paid a lot better than nursing, so porn won out."

"I saw you play a nurse in a movie once."

"Oh, yeah, I play a good naughty nurse."

"Well, thanks, Nina."

"Hey, let me give you my card. I'm always looking for art to dress the set with so there's something to look at besides people fucking."

"Do people need more than that?"

"Not really, but I like it."

She wasn't wearing anything you could carry a business card in, so she waved the P.R. guy over again and he gave me one.

"My address is on there," she said. "Send me some art. Maybe I'll be able use it in a movie."

"Alright, I'll do that."

"I know you will," she said.

There was a small army of creeps queued up behind me, wanting autographs and photos. Nina gave me a kiss on the cheek and signed my *Boogie Nights* soundtrack. *Boogie Nights* was a mainstream Hollywood film in which Nina had a small part, playing a woman in the porn biz who drives her sap of a husband to suicide. She wasn't half bad in it. I thanked her and got out of there, holding the movie over my crotch to hide the hard-on.

I told my wife about it when I got back to the apartment.

"She gave you her business card?"

"Yeah. My paintings in a porn film, think about it. Nina Hartley will be on a couch with all of her orifices filled, cum will be flying, and right there on the wall behind her will be one of my paintings—maybe a nude of *you*."

"Great, our finest hour."

"Ridiculous."

"Nice Polaroid. I like how she inscribed it."

"For Butt Boy, yeah. I'm not sure what that's about."

"She's looking a little long in the tooth."

"Well, yeah, she's in her forties now. But look at what the tooth is attached to."

"I can see what the tooth's attached to, Butt Boy."

"Wanna fuck?"

"I'll race you to the shower," she said.

My wife was elsewhere now, but I still had Nina Hartley's card in my wallet. I opened a bottle of wine and drank it while listening to Elliot Smith records. I fished out Nina's business card. It had a tiny drawing of a naked lady on it. It said, *Nina Hartley: Actress*. There was a mailing address. Her phone number. I opened another bottle of wine and started to put together a package to send her. I rolled up four or five of my paintings and put them in a mailing tube. I put half a dozen erotic drawings in there, and an old watercolor of my wife for good measure. I wrote a long, impaired letter using a ballpoint pen and mentioned that I was drinking wine and listening to sad records but the sad records were too much and I'd better turn them off and I hoped to see my paintings in a skin-flick before I died and that my wife's name was illegible and she had raven black hair and the most beautiful eyes I had ever seen.

I signed the letter, stuck it in the tube with the paintings and drawings, sealed the ends with duct tape, addressed it, pasted an entire book of stamps on, and set it outside my door for the mailman to pick up. I loved that the mailman had a key to the building. It was magic. You licked a stamp, put a piece of yourself in the hall, and the following day it was on its way out and into the world, message-in-a-bottle-like.

I got on the phone and called my wife. It was 4 a.m. She didn't answer. I hung up and smashed my head against the wall hard enough to put a hole through the plaster. *This is going to cost me*, I thought. I felt dizzy. There was blood. The music was loud. I wasn't sure whose music it was. My vision blurred and the room swam away.

I woke up on the floor the following afternoon. The telephone was off the hook, the receiver next to my head. "*Your call cannot be completed as dialed. If you'd like to make a call, please hang up and dial again...Your call cannot...*" I hung up, went to the bathroom, looked in the mirror and said, "Boo." I looked again. "Oh, shit." I heard the mailman in the hall, felt my heart seize, and made a run for the front door. It was one of those beautiful Indian Summer Saturdays when you can't tell if the kids playing in the yard two houses down are having fun or being murdered.

"I need that back!"

The mailman stiffened, wheeled around. "What the hell is wrong with you?"

It was a good question. "Take it," I told him. "Whatever will be will be."

I had a gash on my forehead, blood in my hair. I was in my underwear.

"That's the spirit," he said.

Belt

Work became increasingly difficult each day. I'd arrive like a fragile, nerve-wracked zombie. The slightest sound would make me jump out of my skin, and being a bar, the place was nothing but sound—jam band rock and a normcore clientele screaming for beer and overpriced hamburgers. I'd lost weight. I began using speaker wire to hold my pants up. This did not go unnoticed by my co-workers. I need to buy a belt, I kept thinking. But I hadn't bought anything like that in years and I just never got around to it. Finally, one of the girls I worked with, a little tie-dye wearing wisp of a thing, gave me one of hers.

"This is too small for me," she said.

It was a black leather belt with a square silver buckle. I put it through the loops of my pants, buckled up, and felt five years old again.

"Perfect," she said. Her name was Amy. She looked like Tinkerbell.

"Thanks," I told her. "Do you need any speaker wire?"

At home, my cats picked up on my breakdown vibe. I could see my own grief and fear reflected in their eyes and it hurt me to see them that way. It increased my anxiety, as well as theirs, and they would run around the apartment in frantic zigzags, howling and crashing into walls as if chased by Satan. It was always worse at night. Shortly after the sun went down each day my thoughts would snowball me into flight-mode and the cats would go crazy and I'd grab my keys and get the hell out of there before the walls closed in and swallowed the three of us whole.

I'd always head straight to a bar.

I needed the alcohol to come down. I needed the light and the voices to stay sane and forget who I was and what was happening to me, to my mind. I'd been hospitalized as a teenager, and the thought of needing to be hospitalized again was overwhelming. Only this time, there would be no insurance, no hospital, no home. I never went back to my apartment sober anymore. I often wouldn't remember leaving the bar. I would wake up in my apartment the next day, on the couch, or the kitchen floor, but most of the time in my bed, with my cats using me as a heating pad.

I began to treat my cats more and more like children, rather than the aliens that would attack my brush while I was trying to paint. I was supposed to be a painter, but I didn't paint much anymore. There were a lot of things I didn't do much anymore. I preferred sitting on the couch, smoking pot and petting the cats. Their names were Kook and Bug. We'd sit there together, staring into space all afternoon. I talked to them. Excessively. I figured out their language and they figured out most of mine. They got so accustomed to non-stop attention that they became special needs cats. They were affection junkies. They needed it the way I needed alcohol. "Peace," I'd say to them. And they would purr like mad little motors of joy.

Then the sun would set again.

Tomorrow you will have a panic attack on the train and a police officer will make you breathe into a paper bag.

Focus

I put a beer in his hand and sat him on the couch. "Listen to this," I told him. "It's a recording I made of one of my uncles when I was a kid. Think of it as a radio play. My uncle's name was Dick. He's the guy with the obnoxious voice. There's a guy named Elliot on here too. Elliot is the one who sounds brain damaged." I pressed PLAY and swallowed a Dilaudid.

Elliot: I'll bet you could guess for hours and never figure out where I was goin.

Dick: I wanna ask you something right now. If you're so fuckin intelligent, why are you doin what you're doin today at the Pentwater Wire? Why'd you take my fuckin job away from me?

Elliot: Take your job away?

Dick: Yeah, why'd you do that?

Elliot: What?

Dick: Can you *handle* my job?

Elliot: *Your* job? Where?

Dick: Pentwater Wire!

Elliot: *My* job? I like *my* job.

Dick: Could you handle *my* job?

Elliot:: I could?

Dick: Could you? Can you make a set-up?

Elliot: I could set up.

Dick: I'll tell you what. I'll tear a one-ten down, or one twenty-five, eighteen, twenty-one fuckin guns, electrodes and one-ten—I got better than that—you wanna check it out?

Elliot: I can clean electrodes.

Dick: Fuck, ya don't know how to set the sonofabitch up! Ya don't know what fuckin fixtures to use!

Elliot: I could not do maintenance. But I could set things up.

Dick: Could ya? I'll talk to Jack Relic tomorrow. I need a helper. I got three fuckin guys workin under me now don't know a fuckin thing about a set up. There's only one man that can do a fuckin set up, and that's me. I'm talking about big fuckin machines now. I'm not talking job shop, them little fuckin guns there. I'm talking about twenty-one fuckin guns, or sixteen, or twenty-one fuckin...Hey, *fixtures*, man! I set them fuckers up! I'm the only one can fuckin do it!

Elliot: Oh?

Dick: Ya wanna talk to Mr. Pedder?

Elliot: Who?

Dick: The boss! The president! Mr. Pedder!

Elliot: About what?

Dick: You wanna be a set up man?

Elliot: I could.

Dick: Ya could?

Elliot: It'd be more money than welding.

Dick: I don't think so.

Elliot: I'll earn it somehow. Work my butt off.

Dick: You know what *I* make an hour?

Elliot: Probably six, seven bucks.

Dick: Nooooo, *three-seventy-five*. I'm not in the union yet. I'm not in the *union*.

"This guy's giving me a headache," Marcus said.

"Which guy?"

"Both guys."

I got up and shut it off. I called them the *Dick Tapes*. I had hours of the stuff. I packed a bowl and handed it to Marcus.

"My mother used to say the same thing when I played these tapes back in high school. Dick was one of her brothers. I'd be in my room with my friends, playing this shit and laughing. My mother would always scream at me to turn it off."

"I can see why."

"I played it to you for a reason, but I can't remember now..."

"How's that vitamin D treating you?"

"Vitamin D?"

"The Dilaudid."

"Oh, yeah, vitamin D. I like that. Milk, sure."

"Well?"

"Well what?"

"You want some more or are you good?"

"I'm good, but I'll take some for the future, if you're giving it away."

"Sure, take some." He dumped a small blue mountain of

89

pills onto the coffee table.

"Thanks."

"What was the meaning of that tape? Why'd you play it for me?"

"I don't remember."

"Dick, huh? That's funny. Uncle *Dick*."

"Yeah, he died in the 80s. Abdominal hemorrhage. He was forty-six, forty-seven, I think. Of all my uncles, he was the nicest."

Marcus had craned his neck around and was checking out the wall behind my couch, studying the thing. Some moments passed. Then he said it. I'd been hearing it a lot lately.

"All these photos you have on your wall, it's kind of fucked up."

"We're not divorced yet."

"Why don't you take them down?"

"I like them there."

"You have to move on."

"I may move back to Michigan."

"What, and work at the wire factory?"

"I know. I'm stuck here."

"Why don't you paint anymore?"

"I can't paint. I've tried. I'm a service industry grunt. I'm going to end up in a fucking factory, getting drunk every night after work and having some sixteen-year old kid secretly tape record my conversations for a laugh."

"You're being ridiculous."

"I'm being realistic."

"You have to pull yourself together."

"That's what my wife keeps telling me."

"I thought you weren't going to talk to her for a while."

"She calls, or I call..."

"You're co-dependent. Totally fucking co-dependent."

"What the fuck does that mean?"

"It means you can't live without each other. You're co-dependent."

"What about you?" I said. "Could you live without your wife?"

"You gotta do what you gotta do," he said.

He had a big chunk of Dilaudid hanging from the hairs of

his left nostril.

"It's late," I told him. "You should go say goodnight to your kids."

"Yeah, I guess it's that time, isn't it?"

"Say goodnight, Dick, say goodnight."

"What's that supposed to mean?"

"It's something my uncle used to say."

Laundry Pen

The kid is always trying to feed me. I ate a turkey sandwich he served me about an hour ago. My mistake was the cookie right after. I have the munchies again, but I'm afraid to eat the popcorn he made. I stand and walk around the room, around the room, around the room, before walking into the kitchen and scrawling on his mother's refrigerator the following eight words:

Market Church Prison Whorehouse
Trade Worship Love Murder

You're going to get in trouble for that, he says.

Lou Reed

It felt about ninety-five degrees and the sun was beating down like a big dumb god. I popped a Tic-Tac into my mouth and held the door for her.

"Where should we start, Small Press or Periodicals?"

"Small Press."

"You win the prize."

"What prize?"

"You'll see."

We pointed ourselves toward the Small Press section. I went for the Os and pulled a book off the shelf: *Love Notes On A Public Sign To Kimberly.* I put it in Leticia's hand.

"What's this?"

"It's a book. I'm buying."

"What's it about?"

"I don't know, it's funny."

She flipped the pages. "This is a novel? It doesn't look like a novel."

"It's a decoy," I told her.

She slipped it into her purse.

"What are you doing?" I said, but she was already halfway up the aisle, on her way to the S&M shelf, in Erotica.

"Have you read *Venus in Furs*?" she said.

"No," I told her, "but I know that Lou Reed has."

We walked over to Fellini's for some Greek food. It was dark in there and the bathrooms looked like a speed freak's fevered hallucination.

Leticia spent a lot of time in the Ladies Room. We ordered our food and drinks and off she went.

Five minutes, ten minutes, fifteen...

I finished my drink and started in on hers. I was getting worried. Maybe I should check on her. Maybe she was dead in there. Then she emerged, syrupy slow, like a charmed snake, like all of my darkest wet dreams, toward our table.

She smiled.

"Are you all right?"

"Sure."

"Yeah, you look all right. I'm almost jealous. You want your drink back?"

"No, you keep it."

Our food arrived: hummus, feta, black olives, salad, pita bread.

"I'm not very hungry," she said.

"I thought you were starving."

"I was, but I'm not anymore."

"Have some salad," I told her.

She began picking apart the salad with her fingers, popped an olive into her mouth.

Her hair was long and dark, rail-straight, Nefertiti-like. Her eyes were shinny little pinpoints. "Olives are good," she said.

I ate everything on both of our plates while she picked at the salad. I ordered another drink. "Wanna get out of here?" I said.

"Yeah, show me where you live."

I slammed my drink and we got out of there.

Stay

I sleep fourteen hours a day and eat nothing but chocolate. Drink a sea of coffee. It doesn't help. Nothing keeps me awake these days, which is odd, because I've been an insomniac most of my life. I used to watch TV all night. Wait for the morning to come, for the fear to pass. There was a brief period of time when I was neither sleepy nor an insomniac. That time no longer exists.

I still have a TV, not that it works anymore. Loose wire, blown tube—who knows? I can't say that I've ever understood machines. The how and why of the way things work.

I haven't stopped looking at it though. In the afternoon, I'll sit on the couch and see myself reflected fish-eyed in the glass. See my living room, the floor, the ceiling, three of the four walls. Coffee table piled high with unopened mail, old vacation photos, half-read books, ash tray overflowing with cigarette butts. The foil of Hershey's Kisses blown around like shrapnel. Me, in the center of it all, this catastrophe. I can look at that thing for hours, that person there. I'm always amazed that it's me. How can that be me? Sometimes, I'll crawl across the floor for a closer look. Yeah, that's me alright: My show, My situation. Sometimes I think I must have mono, or maybe cancer. Some sort of cancer.

I've never much cared for what is shown on TV, but for as long as I can remember, there's always been one around. And I've always watched it. Me and billions of others. TV Babies. People too young to remember a world without TV, people who were born into it. Our numbers are growing larger every minute of every day. Pretty soon there won't be anyone who remembers that other world.

My wife is a TV Baby. But she tells me she doesn't own one anymore, and that she doesn't miss it.

This TV doesn't even work. But I can't bring myself to drag it to the dumpster. That would be a form of suicide, wouldn't it? Nothing left to reflect me—my living room, couch, coffee table—nothing left to tell me who and where I am. What I am. Then again, that might be good. Might be just what I need. But I would feel more alone, I think, might lose sight of myself, altogether. I need to be reminded, yes.

So the TV stays.
The TV stays after all else has vanished.
Me and the TV, we stay.

Something

I got a phone call from my ex. I was on the couch with my cats.

"Hello?"

"Hi, it's me."

"Hey, how are you?"

"Where have you been?"

"Right here."

"No you haven't. I've been trying to get a hold of you for days."

"I've been around—why?"

"I've been worried. I came looking for you last night. I thought you were dead."

"Why would I be dead?"

"Something's going on with you."

"What?"

"You sound funny. Are you on something?"

"Am I *on* something?"

"That message you left was fucking lame."

"What message?"

"You know what message."

I looked at the hole in the wall above the phone stand. Something stirred my memory, rolled over and groaned. I scratched the scab on my forehead, felt the goose egg there, guilt. "Listen, whatever I said, I'm sorry, alright?"

"You made it sound like you were going to kill yourself. You were saying goodbye."

"I was drunk. I didn't mean it. I'm sorry."

"You're drunk a lot."

"I'm sad."

"I was in your apartment last night."

"What were you doing in my apartment?"

"I was looking for you. I still have the keys, remember? I thought you were dead in there."

"I was alive, elsewhere."

"You got a call from Nina Hartley."

"What?"

"Last night, while I was sitting in your apartment, fucking

crying, she called."

"What did she want?"

"She wanted to *talk* to you."

"About what?"

"Your paintings or something. I don't know, *I was crying.*"

"What do you mean, you were crying?"

"I looked all over town for you. I called everyone!"

"I was fine."

"You hadn't been home in days. Craig told me so."

Craig was my apartment manager. He lived in the unit above mine. His floor was my ceiling. He drank and liked music and never bothered me about the rent being late.

"Sometimes I don't go home," I told her.

"Are you seeing someone?"

"What do you care?"

"Where do you go?"

"I have friends. I'm not a hermit."

"She's really nice."

"Who?"

"Nina Hartley, she was nice."

"Yeah?"

"She was really supportive."

"Supportive of what?"

"She could hear I was upset. We talked."

"Talked about what?"

"She helped me calm down."

"What exactly did you talk about?"

"*You, that message—everything!*"

"Okay, I understand."

"*Do you?*" she said.

"Do you have to *italicize* everything?"

"*Fuck you!*"

"Did she say she'd call back?"

There was the sound of smashing glass, and the line went dead. I reached for a ballpoint pen, snatched a piece of paper from the floor.

Dear Nina...

Robot

I'm on the train today (no, yesterday, my circadian cycle's off, can't sleep) sitting behind three teenagers. They're talking about going to a party later, all excited about it, and one of them says, "Oh, wait, I told Lori I'd hang out with her tonight."

The other two give him shit. "Lame! Lame!"

The kid says, "I promised!"

One of the kids says, "Okay, whatever."

The other kid knocks his hat off and says, "Girlfriends are gay!"

"Yeah," I say. They turn around to see who said that. "SUPER gay," I say.

They all look at each other—"WTF?"—turn back around.

"Super DUPER gay," I say.

Their stop comes and they get up to go. Two of them give me the stink eye as they pass. The kid Lori wants to bang looks at me sideways, big grin on his face.

It's the little things, sure.

Later, at work, I watch a five-year old draw a robot while his parent's drink coffee.

"Pretty cool," I say. "How much?"

"Nothin."

He laughs, tears the edges off, hands it to me.

"Hey, wait, that's way too much. I don't have that kind of cash, kid."

"Nothin's less than nothin!" he says.

"You're right," I tell him. "I'll take it."

Can't sleep. Can't sleep.

One long Today. Big! Mind boggling!

Circadian cycle, kaput. Blue triangles. (Mean standard!)

Time to board the train again.

Hard

I adored her but she had let her cat starve while running around who knows how long scoring dope and doing what?

I had just given her a Xanax and an orange, though I'd never seen her eat. Benzos, sleeping pills. She would come around for that shit when short on what she really needed, which was something I had the taste but not the tolerance for. I had all those pills because my doctor was insane. I had a doctor because I had insurance. But the insurance was running out.

"Got any pills?" she'd say.

I sometimes did but didn't always say so.

"No. Well, maybe," I'd say. Even if I didn't. Even if I did.

She didn't tell me how her cat died. Someone else did. No food. No water. Weeks passing. I never called her on it because I was afraid it might be true.

"No way," she said. "Not until you give me Nina Hartley's phone number."

"What do you want with Nina Hartley's phone number?"

"I'm thinking of moving back to Los Angeles."

"And?"

"Porn, dummy!"

"Oh."

I didn't want her to go. LA would be the end of her. And yes, I'd miss her.

"I need to get clean," she said. "I wanna go stay with my mom for awhile and kick."

"You're going to live with your mom, do porn, and kick?"

"Just give me her number."

"It's on my machine."

"She left you a message?"

"Yeah." I'd been too afraid to listen to it beyond the beep and the hi.

I had Nina's business card in my wallet, but I always hid my wallet when Leticia came around.

She moved from the couch to my answering machine, which was hooked to a land line I was too flattened to have much to do with. The answering machine had been a gift. The ancient god of a past employer. Thus it came to me.

"It says you have forty-eight messages on here. I'm not going to listen to all this shit."

"Suit yourself."

"Oh for fuck sake."

She pressed PLAY and the voices came.

Blah, blah, blah. Blah, blah, blah. Yo, buddy. Blah blah blah. You there? Blah, blah, blah...

"Hey, that's me! Why didn't you call back?"

"I never heard it."

BEEP

"That's me again!"

"Never heard it."

BEEP

"Again!"

"Never heard it."

BEEP

"Aw, your mother."

"Shit, I need to call her."

"You're a horrible son. You know that, right?"

BEEP

A voice said, "Hey, it's Nina!"

Holy shit!

I got up and went to the bathroom to pee, thought about Nina Hartley, all that 70s and 80s porn of my repressed suburban youth, got half hard hearing her voice on the machine, felt weird about it, flushed.

"She likes the painting you sent her."

"Why?"

"She wants you to send more so she can use them in a movie."

I zipped up and walked back to the living room.

"That's funny," I said.

"Would she pay you?"

"Did you get her number?"

"Yeah."

"Good. I should probably get ready for work."

"Why didn't you try to fuck me last night?"

"You told me you were tired."

"That doesn't stop other guys."

101

I felt dumb and embarrassed.

She grabbed her purse, got up to go.

Always getting up, always going, going, gone. Like all of us, I guess.

When I was twenty-one, a woman got angry with me because I couldn't fuck her while a guy who claimed to be her brother sat drinking beer in the kitchen. "You're confused," she said. I backed away and began putting on my clothes.

"But you're hard!" the woman screamed. Her shoes rocketing across the room, deranging the walls, dogging my head for days.

Wimp Son Pandemic

Turn a corner down the heart of it
Teddy bear sitting in a shopping cart squat with coats shoes
shirts and trash
Tarp stuffed up front spilling to the street
Matching blue box of CRAZY GOOD COOKIES AND
CREAM (NO MATTER HOW YOU LOVE 'EM)
standing at the base of it all
Teddy Bear USA.
Dollar store water bottle between its legs
Instant soup cup crushed against its hip
Pizza box at the back of the neck.
Woman in a blanket on the sidewalk: "You like the teddy
bear? You can borrow him if you want."
Take a picture.
"Go ahead, borrow it."
Crows everywhere diving surfing swimming sounding
Big noise.
Move along.
Full moon means rent is due.
Fills you with dread.

He's Wearing a Green Shirt, That Means He's Growing, No, Not Growing, He's Regressing, He's Green, He's Growing— No, He's Going, He's Going Away

him very ill

afternoon of 27 July
a pistol

One of his last words

moments later

Office of the Dead
the cemetery
was covered with yellow
sun

Roman Candle

"How you doing?"

I was sitting on the roof of my apartment building with Danny. We had eaten two grams too many mushrooms about thirty minutes prior to climbing the tree that allowed us to get onto the roof.

"I feel weird," I told him.

"You'll be feeling weirder, soon."

"No, I feel weird about being up here. Too visible."

"No one's looking up here."

"It seems like a bad idea."

"Relax, dude. Check out those stars."

I checked them out. Orion was up there, the Big Dipper, the Little Dipper. There were certainly more, but Orion and the Dippers were the only constellations I had ever been able to identify. The moon was low on the horizon, red and swollen. Danny was wearing a trucker hat with the word *SECURITY* printed above the bill.

"I'm worried about how I'm going to pay my rent this month," I told him.

"You'll make it."

"I don't know."

"Did you see that shooting star?"

"What shooting star?"

"You didn't see that shooting star?"

"No, I didn't see it."

"It was a good one. I can't believe you missed that.

"I think I'm going to end up homeless one day."

"Oh, come on, man."

"Homeless and alone. It's inevitable."

"Dude, you're tripping. It's all part and parcel of the whole."

"Which hole?"

"What?"

"I don't know what you're saying."

"You're tripping, dude."

I walked to the edge of the roof, peered over. We were two and a half stories up. I looked at the moon. There seemed to be something fundamentally wrong with it. I walked back to where Danny was sitting.

"I have to get off this building," I told him.

"We just got here."

"I'm going down."

"Chill, man, it's nice up here."

"Where the hell is the tree we climbed?"

He made a vague motion with his hand.

"What's that supposed to mean?"

"It's over there somewhere." He pointed to a dark corner of the roof.

I took baby steps toward the top of the tree. I stood there awhile, staring at it. It was swaying, changing shape, glowing. I grabbed a branch. I stood there some more. Then I swung on in.

"OH JESUS GOD!"

Ninety minutes later, I was on solid ground again.

I went back to my apartment. Everything looked crazy in there. Even the cats looked crazy. I picked up the phone and dialed 911.

"Hello?"

I didn't say anything.

"Hello? This is 911."

I was paralyzed.

"Is this an emergency? Hello?"

I hung up. I moved toward the stereo, put some music on, and paced around the living room in circles for a while. A voice came out of the speakers.

"*The strangest thing happened to me on the way to outer space today.*"

I walked over to one of the speakers and stared at it.

"*Just let me love you,*" the voice sang.

I stood there, staring, until the music stopped. I felt peaceful, benevolent, slightly insane.

My cats were staring at me.

"Come on, babies, time to go to sleep."

We crawled into bed and situated ourselves.

There was a tremendous pounding at the door. I leapt up and sent the cats flying.

"Who is it?"

"It's Danny, open up!"

I opened the door and Danny walked in, saucer-eyed, his hat in his hand. He had recently shaved his hair off and his forehead appeared freakishly large. Insectile. E.T.-like. Fuck!

"You should put your hat back on," I told him.

"I saw something up there." he said.

"Up where?"

"On the roof. I fell into my head. I think I saw the men behind the curtain! The men at the controls!"

"Keep your voice down. I have neighbors." It was true. My stoner landlord lived in the apartment directly above mine, and there was a woman one door down named Annie something or another, an aging ex-dancer who routinely clawed at the other side of my bedroom wall late at night while weeping. Some nights, we'd both be weeping. I felt bad for my landlord.

Danny walked over to the telephone and began dialing.

"IS THIS AN EMERGENCY?" I said.

My cats where staring at him.

He put the phone down. He looked at Kook, he looked at Bug, he looked at me. Six pairs of eyes boring holes in his forehead.

"I have to get out of here." he said.

"Time is a perfect zero," I told him, "something to push your finger through."

He disappeared, left the door wide open.

Kook made a break for it but I caught him before he could escape.

"You don't want to go out there," I told him.

Trespass. Satellite. Flying eye.
HELLO.

It came out of my speakers like a freight train.

It was time to wake up. That's what the clock said.

I got out of bed, walked into the living room and turned my stereo off. The sun was up, casting garish shadows. The world and my place in it always looked shittier in the full light of day. But I felt relatively okay for a change. I hadn't had that much to drink the night before. Xanax and 'shrooms, maybe it was the safer path. Ben and Jerry's or black leather? Tough call. There were urban hipsters and there were Hawthorne hippies and boy you didn't want to be caught on the wrong side of that line. Nah.

I fed the cats and put on a pot of coffee. I put some bread in the toaster. I had some cream cheese in the fridge. I sat on the couch and drank my coffee and smoked a cigarette and thought about the toast and the cream cheese and my stance on the urban hipster vs. Hawthorne hippie situation. I didn't have the energy to think about it for more than sixty seconds, so I turned the TV on and jammed some toast and cream cheese into my mouth.

I only got two channels and they were fuzzy at best, but I was watching one of them, and they were showing footage of a tall, impressive building stabbing the sky and spewing flame like a Roman candle. I took a closer look.

New York!

As I was watching the newsman talk, I saw a plane flying into a second building, which could be seen just over the guy's right shoulder. He wheeled around and saw it too. He seemed flustered, working without a script. I listened for awhile, but I can't remember what he talked about. I got up and walked into my kitchen and looked out the window. It was a full on glorious September morning, the sun blasting down its ultra violet. I could see Mount Hood, and the Willamette River, and the SUVs forming a long winding snake up and down the freeway, people on their way to work, everything rolling along to schedule.

I got dressed and took my time searching for change for the bus. I figured they'd cut me a few minutes slack that morning. I usually worked the night shift.

"You're five minutes late," my manager said. The television behind her head showed the World Trade Center collapsing, from different angles, in replay after replay.

"Write me up," I told her.

She wrote me up. Nothing felt very real in the 21st century. Not even reality. Reality felt like the least real thing of all.

I went about my business of opening the bar. The rest of the crew stood there looking at the television. It was the same whenever there was a football game on. I was the only idiot working because I was the only one who wasn't interested in the game or who won or lost the goddamn game.

Five minutes late. Never six. And the world is always burning.

I set-up the bar while my coworkers stared at the symbolic collapse of Western Civilization. I went into the walk-in and cracked a beer and sat there, shivering in the cold, drinking it.

Aggro-Hippie Handing Out Trail-Mix on the Max

Remember that time you tried to bash my head in with a rock?
No.
That wasn't you?
No.
You sure?
Yes.
You want some trail-mix?
I'm good.

Easy to Lose

I'm turning over the contents of my wallet to the naked spirits at Mary's, the oldest strip club in Portland. It's a shady landmark and so am I—shitfaced, suicidal, dreading the arrival of closing time, reckoning, the end of the ride. I'm afraid to go home. There's nothing there. I'm always afraid to go home. Tonight the feeling is magnified ten-fold. There's a guy sitting next to me at the rail who's been tipping nothing but twenties for the last three hours. It's Christmas Eve, crashing into Christmas day.

"LAST CALL!"

I order one last whatever I can afford and toss the remainder of my cash onto the stage. The spirit laughs as she scoops it up. She's beautiful, lovely, galaxies beyond me. The guy sitting next to me taps my shoulder and screams into my face: "Where the fuck can you get a drink in this town?" Red hair, baseball hat, big ears, nose full of broken blood vessels.

I tell him the bars stop serving at 2 a.m.

"All of 'em?" he says, blue eyes, bad teeth. "Follow me. I'm staying at [fancy hotel]. We'll hit the mini-bar."

"Right," I say, and stagger after him. Stagger Lee. Good Seattle band, now dismembered. I hum one of their tunes while trying to walk a straight line.

It's cold out but the hotel is close. We get there and blue eyes tips the doorman forty dollars. He tips the elevator operator, waves to the desk clerk. They all smile and seem to know him: Mr. Big Bucks. I flop down on a couch in a suite way up high with the pigeons and the stars and tell Big Bucks I'd like a vodka tonic. We make small talk, about drinks and drinking, small drunk talk.

"I made six million dollars this year," he tells me. He dials the phone and when the bellhop arrives he gives him a handful of cash and sends him off to get drugs. I didn't know you could do that. I don't know a lot of things.

"What's your story?" I ask. But I'm not really interested. I have a drink in my hand.

"Six million dollars," he says. "I tried twice and failed. This third time, I got lucky. I started a thing on the internet, then I sold it. Now I'm a consultant. I'm on my way to Seattle.

Wanna go?"

"I have a job to be at. I didn't make six million dollars this year."

"Fuck it. How much do you make? What do you do?"

"We're characters in a bad movie," I tell him. "I'm a bartender."

"Come up to Seattle for a few days. I'll put five grand in your bank account right now. We'll hang out and get fucked up."

"Right."

"I'm serious. I'll give you five grand! What's your account number?"

"Fuck that."

The bellhop raps on the door and Big Bucks gets up to let him in. They do their business and I fix myself another drink from the mini-bar. Big Bucks tips the kid sixty dollars, twenty, twenty, twenty, quick in the palm, shuts the door and tells me all about it.

"All he could find was crack," he says, and sits down and hooks himself up an empty Coke can to smoke it from. "You want some?"

"I hate that shit," I tell him. I've never tried it. Don't intend to.

"You'll want some later." He gets up and turns on the television: Cable porn. No penetration.

I go to the bathroom. I check my eyes, splash water on my face, spit into the mirror like it's some stupid movie.

When I get back, Big Bucks has a chair pulled up close to the TV. He has his pants off and he's trying to masturbate.

"I love this chick," he says. But he can't get it up. His piggly wiggly dick is useless. He keeps working at it, breaking every few strokes to bring the Coke can to his mouth. His dick lays there like one of those dead worms you see on the sidewalk after a hard rain. I close one eye and look at the TV. The smell of the crack reminds me of a cancer ward, dead relatives, open wounds. The woman on the TV is beautiful. I know her but I can't remember her name.

"God," Big bucks says, "I wanna fuck her. Are you bi?"

I tell him no. I stare at the TV. I'm no good with names.

"I think I'm bi," he says.

It strikes me as funny to think I was once married and in love, that I used to eat meals and go for walks and kiss my wife goodnight and not feel terrified on the holidays, so funny I want to cry. But that will come later, when I get back to my apartment. The sun will be streaming through the windows and I'll want to be dead. Not that it matters now. I pick up the Coke can, put a rock in there, and fill my lungs with chemicals, exhaling a noxious cloud of hopelessness. Six million dollars. Money can buy just about anything. But it's not enough. Big Bucks probably won't live long enough to spend it all. Or worse, he will.

"Can I suck your dick?" he says.

I tell him no. He fiddles with his lighter.

I lay down on a love seat, and let Big Bucks do his drugs. The crack makes my brain feel like a pinball machine. I close my eyes. Why is crack so much easier to find at 4 a.m. than weed? Because the dealers are using and the stoners are all asleep. I have some Xanax in my pocket. I take two, let them dissolve under my tongue, slip in and out of bad dreams. Hours seem to pass. I lift one eye and see Big Bucks squatting in front of the TV, blue flickering light, shadows, people fucking. He's squatting over a hotel towel, sticking mini-bar bottles up his ass, still smoking crack, still no hard-on.

I sit up, collect myself. I'm clean now, pure of heart, half crazed. "Hey, you know that magazine you brought back from the club? You can call someone. There's a whole section in the back, photos, numbers, everything."

"No shit? Call someone!" He pauses before pulling a bottle out of his ass. "I hope this isn't freaking you out."

"Hey, listen, I'm out of cigarettes."

"There's some money on the table," he says. "Take a ten. Get a couple packs, Camel Lights." He turns his face back to the TV. I page through the magazine. It's called *Exotica*. The people are called "escorts." There's a pile of cash sitting on the end table by the door, hundred dollar bills, fifty dollar bills, twenties, tens, fives. I have a vision of myself lighting it all on fire but I don't. Or do I? I grab enough to catch a bus and I leave—out the door, up the hallway, into an elevator, down, off the elevator, through a lobby where I wave to a soldier in a Santa Claus suit, out another door and into the street. The sun is up, bright, alarming, unreal. The morning air hits my face, big blue car wreck of a world, alarms, bells, gasoline smells, and the Christmas people are awake, making their way to where? A hot meal with family and friends, presents and ham and mashed potatoes with gravy, cookies and gingerbread houses and eggnog minus the booze, or too much of it, or home to none of this, simply home.

They all have stories. They are all full of secrets. I'd tell mine to god, if I believed there was a god. I think a god would understand.

Kiss Kids on Heroin

In a borrowed car, driving downtown to score some food at the diner we both abhor and adore. It's raining so hard it's impossible to tell how fast we're going.

On the way there, you glare at me and say, "So, we're divorced, huh?"

"Almost."

"Are you damaged now?"

"What?"

"Are you broken? Do you feel that you can never love again?"

I'm taken aback. No one has ever asked me this.

"I'm not sure," I say. "I hope not."

"I've felt that way before."

"Oh, yeah?"

"Sure."

"Do you still feel that way?"

"No."

"What changed it?"

"I found another girl," you say, your eyes shiny little pinpoints, the only stars in town.

I stick my head out the passenger window and see that we aren't even driving on a road.

"Stick your head out the window all you want," you tell me. "You still can't see tomorrow."

I take off my coat, sit down, hear a knock at my door, stand up, open the door.

It's Gene Simmons, of the band Kiss.

"What are you doing here?"

"I thought I'd stop by and check up on you."

"Check up on me?"

"Yeah."

He pushes me aside, walks on his platform boots across the clutter of my living room—pill bottles and your blackened spoons—picks up a crayon and draws the Kiss logo on the wall above my television.

"Hey, this is a rental, you can't do that!"

"But you *love* Kiss."

"Yeah, when I was 14. I'm 46 now."

"I'm 62."

"Yes?"

"I still get all the pussy."

I got nothing, it seems, and nothing to say to that.

"Young pussy," he says.

"Okay..."

"Really young," he says.

"I've read that," I say.

"It defies logic," he laughs. But does it?

"And you?" he says.

"Me what?"

"You never got any in High School. I've read about you, too."

"No you haven't."

"You're right, I haven't. That's because you don't get the pussy."

A pause ensues and seems to last nine months.

He pats his codpiece, sizing me up. "Everything seems to be in order here, Mister Eisenlohr. Carry on."

"Will do," I say. And poof, he disappears in a cloud of stage smoke, a smattering of applause.

I sit down, open a book, read the first line:

"Long before love there was solitude."

Another knock at the door: Me, you posing as me, my mirror.

"Hey, how you doing?"

"You! Thank God!"

"What?"

"Gene Simmons was just here."

"*Thee* Gene Simmons?"

"Yeah, the guy from Kiss."

"What did he want?"

"I'm not sure."

"Nice Kiss logo you have on your wall, dork."

"I didn't put that there, he did."

"Remember that song *Christine Sixteen*?"

"Yes. I wish I could forget it."

"Got any cereal?"

"I'm all out."

"What about hot dogs?"

"I do have hot dogs."

"Get 'em going. Star Trek is on in five minutes."

"The original series?"

"Of course."

We sit and eat hot dogs, watch Star Trek. "The Way to Eden" episode. I'm wearing pajamas. I'm Japanese, a soldier unaware the war is long over, look at you through thick glasses that Ginger has fogged.

"I didn't know you liked Star Trek," I say.

"Who said I did?"

"Then why are we watching it?"

"I never said I *didn't* like it."

"Want another hot dog?"

"You know what I always say."

"What's that?"

"Smoke 'em if you got 'em!" we scream.

You stand, walk to the door, look back and say, "Everything seems to be in order here, lover."

"Don't go," I beg. And poof, I'm alone again.

The trick is to be an absence. The trick is not to be.

It's tricky, isn't it, babe?

Your Issue is Too Serious to Not Be Funny

Also Out On Far West

farwestpress.com

CPSIA information can be obtained
at www.ICGtesting.com
Printed in the USA
BVHW032121190921
617041BV00007B/11

9 781736 538852